I0570585

SAIL AWAY
ON MY
SILVER DREAM

J GUENTHER

WYZARD HILL PRESS

☽ 🜍 ☾

SAIL AWAY ON MY SILVER DREAM
Copyright © 2010, 2012, 2018, by J Guenther
Published by Wyzard Hill Press, Palos Verdes, California

No part of this publication may be reproduced, stored in a retrieval system, or transmitted in any form or by any means, electronic, mechanical, photocopying, recording, or otherwise, without the prior written permission of the copyright owner.

This book is sold subject to the condition that it shall not, by way of trade or otherwise, be lent, resold, hired out, or otherwise circulated without the publisher's prior consent in any form of binding or cover other than that in which it is published and without a similar condition including this condition being imposed on the subsequent purchaser. Under no circumstances may any part of this book be photocopied for resale.

This is a work of fiction. Any similarity between the characters and situations within its pages and places or persons, living or dead, is unintentional and co-incidental.

For information contact:

https://JGuentherAuthor.WordPress.com

Book and cover design by J Guenther. Typeset in

CrimsonSemiBold.otf: Copyright (c) 2010, Sebastian Kosch (sebastian@aldusleaf.org), with Reserved Font Name "Crimson."

Delius-Regular.ttf: Copyright (c) 2010 by Natalia Raices. All rights reserved.

PatrickHandSC-Regular.ttf: Copyright (c) 2010-2012 Patrick Wagesreiter (mail@patrickwagesreiter.at)

CinzelDecorative-Black.ttf: Copyright 2012 Natanael Gama (info@ndiscovered.com), with Reserved Font Name "Cinzel."

Printed in the United States of America
ISBN: 9780997450330
Second Edition: 2019

10 9 8 7 6 5 4 3 2

CC0 public domain sailing ship image via pixabay
Cover image licensed from Adobe Stock

Dedications

To my teachers:

> Gibson Reaves, Richard Condon, Dr. Julia McCorkle, Jeff Hoppenstand, Edith Battles, Anne Lowenkopf, Glad Esther Mitchell, Bill Barnett, Judy Sanger, Mrs. Keshishian, and all the others.

Special thanks to:

> David Kenney, the entire South Bay Writers Workshop of bygone days, Surfwriters, the Palos Verdes writing workshop, Southwest Manuscripters, and Writers of Kern, especially Peggy Connelly and Joe Tomasi.

CHAPTER 1
CLOUDS

The first scary thing happened on Saturday, a week before school started. It was really hot that day. I was in the backyard, using the weed trimmer and getting all sweaty and covered with shredded grass. Mom had her long, brown hair done up in a bandana and was wearing her grubby jeans, cutting roses beside the garden shed. I saw her straighten up, and then she dropped her clippers and just stood there like a statue. Something was wrong with the way she was standing. I stopped what I was doing and wondered, *What's the matter with Mom?*

I was too scared to say anything. I'd never seen her do that before. After maybe ten seconds, she looked at me and said, "David, I've got to go inside and lie down for a minute." She dropped the roses and her gloves and went straight in the back door without putting anything away.

After that, I was too upset to stay outside. I wanted to check and see if she was okay, so I ran around the rest of the yard as fast as I could, lopping off just the tallest weeds. Then I tossed everything into the garden shed and ran into the house. Mom was already asleep on the couch in the den, sort of all curled up. She seemed smaller, somehow. I stood in the doorway, looking at her for a long time, thinking, *Is she all right? What if she isn't?* That was too frightening to think about.

I wanted to go get Dad, but he was over at Grandma's with my little brother, Jason, so I went upstairs and played computer games to take my mind off Mom until Dad got back.

Mom seemed better when she woke up, and I stopped being worried. After dinner, we all went shopping to get my school supplies —a new backpack, a pack of three-hole paper, a new ruler, some pencils, an eraser, a three-ring binder, a new calculator, and some slick folders with superheroes on them. Jason thought he should get something, too, so Mom bought him a floating plastic duck.

I asked her, "Can I get another game for my computer?"

Dad jumped in before Mom could answer. "You've already got too many."

I thought there was no such thing as too many games, but I knew better than to say that. "Most of mine are real old, Dad."

Dad put his foot down. "No more games. End of discussion."

"What about a basketball, instead? Jason can play with it too."

I didn't really plan to let him play with it much, but that was enough to convince Mom. "Shooting baskets in the park with your brother would be better than sitting in your room," she said.

Dad agreed, and I got the basketball.

Everything seemed all right after that. I forgot about the time in the backyard. But I guess now maybe I'd better tell you who I am and that kind of thing.

CHAPTER 1½
WHO AM I?

My name is David Zane Greene, with an *e*. (When I was four or five, I thought my dad's name was Don Greene Withany. That's what I thought I heard him say when he met people. "I'm Don Greene, with-an-e.") I have a little brother, Jason. He's okay. He's just a kid. He was four when all this stuff happened. He's cute, but he can be a humongous pest at times, you know?

I'm starting 7th grade soon, but the things I'll tell you about happened when I was in 5th over a year ago. We were living in what I'll call Rogersville. I won't tell you its real name, and I won't tell you where we live now. It's safer if I don't.

My dad is a designer. He designs machines and appliances of all kinds. He's really smart. He and my mom came from Pennsylvania. She'd been working as a hotel assistant manager back there, but when they moved to Rogersville, I was born and she stopped working to stay home with me. Jason was born there too, about seven years after me.

I don't know if I'll be an engineer like my dad or not. Maybe. I like to read, and I like computers. But right now, I think I'd like to be a therapist, like Dr. Appelman.

Which gets me to why I'm writing this. It was Dr. Appelman's idea. He said it would help me if I put everything down on paper. But I'm also doing this so I won't forget the important things—things about my friend, Sharon, and how we sailed together on the *Silver Dream*. I've changed her name in here, too.

I remember a lot of what we said when we talked, but not all of it, so I've sort of filled in the rest as near as I can recall it.

Sharon was the best friend I've ever had. This is her story, too, and she should be writing it instead of me, but she's not here to do the writing.

One great thing is that Sharon kept a diary. She left it for me to read, and I think it's okay for me to put pieces of it in here. I'm going to leave some personal stuff out, but I'm not going to add or change anything but a few names. It's really going to be Sharon talking to you, like she's telling her own story. (Have you ever wondered what girls put in their diaries? Now's your chance to find out.)

I'll start with Sharon's first entry, about two weeks before school started. She was feeling unhappy about her birthday.

CHAPTER 2
BIRTHDAYS AND BEGINNINGS

August 29: Dear diary, why do people say "Dear diary?" There's nothing dear about a diary. It's just an empty book. I'm going to make this as if I'm writing to a real person, which is more fun. So:

Dear Filbert,

Ha, ha! Just kidding. I wouldn't want a boy to read this. Especially not one named after a nut. I'll call you "Millicent." I think a girl named Millicent would wear fancy hats and expensive shoes. She'd have hair that's long and blonde, instead of short and dark, like mine. She wouldn't ride in an old, beat-up, tan Oldsmobile like my father's; she'd have her own Jaguar. A dark green one that she'd call her "Jag-u-ar."

I don't wear hats much and I'd much rather go barefoot than wear shoes, even expensive ones. And I sure don't have a Jag-u-ar. If I did, I'd be a thousand miles from here!

But it would be interesting to have a friend named Millicent. She'd live a life that's very, very different from me. She'd live in a big city, far away, maybe by the ocean, and she'd have a real father, one who doesn't get drunk all the time and yell at her and her mother. So:

Dear Millicent, for my birthday, I got some socks and underwear (new) and a pair of awful, old waffle-stomper shoes (used, from the thrift store, but they've got only one big scuff mark). They're sort of orangey-colored. Ick! They won't match anything else I have, but they fit and will be okay if I don't grow too fast for a while. I also got a large chocolate bar (I think it's from Factory Super Goof Store, so it could be a bazillion years old). I also got some lame books (*Charlotte Sleuthe, Girl Detective*—very used, and not about elves or unicorns or sailboats or any of the things I like), and this diary (new). Big whoop. No offense, Millicent. The diary is nice.

I wasn't very thrilled, but Mother said this was the best we can do because **he** hasn't found a job since we moved here. I know she had thirty dollars saved up, but *he* found it and spent it. (She didn't tell me about the money, but I heard them yelling about it after I went to bed.)

I know Mother tried really hard. I guess I should have pretended to be happier with the stuff she got me.

Christmas will be better. If not, well, I'll try to be more grateful for anything Mother gives me. Maybe he'll have a job by then. Of course, if I know him, he'll find a way to screw Christmas up, too! He's very creative. I may have to try a *lot* harder to be a cheery little elf at Christmas.

About the time Sharon had her cheapo birthday, our family was just getting back from vacation. We'd driven to Montana that year in Mom's almost-new red SUV. That was really nice! Even my little brother Jason had fun. At least he whined a lot less than usual, so I guess he was having fun.

On the trip, Dad let me use his old camera, and I took pictures everywhere we went. I have a great picture of Mom and Dad and Jason and me in front of the little cabin we stayed in. That's the shot I like the best, even though somebody else took the picture so we could all be in it. It's the only one from Montana with all four of us together. Mom is smiling and healthy. You'd never know she was getting sick.

Montana was a happy time for us. Things went downhill after that for a long time.

I'm not a great reader. Sharon always loved to read a lot, especially fantasy books about elves. And goblins.

September 4: Dear Millicent, Mother took me downtown today. I asked if I could wait in the used bookstore while she shopped for grocs. She knows Mrs. Keshishian, the bookstore lady, so she said okay. Mrs. Keshishian let me swap five Charlotte Sleuthes for four Elfin-Trek books. That was very kind of her. Now I'll have something to read at night. When I'm reading about elves, I'm far, far away, Mill.

September 6: I stayed up really late to finish the first Elfin-Trek book. It was such a good read. The title is *Elf-Lord Lamorien vs. The Goblin King*. The goblin king reminds me of somebody, Millicent. Can you guess who? Right—my father. The goblin king got what he deserved in the end, but it was exciting right up to the last page, when he fell into a deep, deep, pit. If only.

September 9: Finished the second book, *Elves Across the Wide Ocean*. It was about the Elf-Lord's voyage to different kinds of elves in strange lands. He traveled completely around their world, making treaties to protect everybody from evil creatures.

I was an elf for a few hours while I was reading that book, Mill. Elves always seem happy, no matter what. They worry a little about the goblins and the trolls and gnomes, but they know everything is going to be all right. They don't cry when they go to bed at night.

I'd already gotten a bunch of new stuff for school, and the basketball, like I said earlier. Sharon didn't get a heck of a lot.

September 12: Dear Millicent, school tomorrow. My mother brought home a few pencils, a used eraser, and a ball-point pen. From work. They all say "Hardy Tech-a-Temp Agency." She said the manager let her have them free.

I'm not exactly thrilled about starting at another new school. This makes five schools in three years. I get all gurgly in my stomach just thinking about school tomorrow. I'm sure I'll be wearing what all the dweebazoid girls wear. I've outgrown all my stuff from last year except for a pair of barf-colored jeans that I can barely get into. I've got a sweater and a couple of tops that aren't too bad.

Mother insisted on cutting my hair instead of taking me downtown to the hair dresser's. I guess I didn't look dorky enough for her. My bangs look like they were done with a hedge trimmer! I had a fit when I saw myself in the mirror. My mother wasn't too pleased with that.

Maybe I can talk her into getting me a new outfit Friday, so I can fit in. And maybe pigs will fly Friday, too. I'll wear whatever I've got. The weird jeans won't look great with my orange waffle-stompers, but I'll pretend that's ultra hot fashion where I come from. I guess I could tell them I'm from California, which is sort of true, Mill. We lived there six years ago, but they don't need to know that, do they?

PS: The chocolate bar was all powdery on top and had melted in places, so it just says "ersh" on it. It's still edible, so I guess I shouldn't complain. I'll take the rest of it to school with me for emergency purposes, like if I get really bummed.

My father didn't come home Saturday night. We're not sure exactly where he was. Mother went out sometime in the night to look for him, but no luck . . . if finding a drunk could be lucky. He snuck in without saying anything in time for lunch. He didn't look too hot. Neither did she, now that I think about it.

Speaking of *him*, I finished the third book, *Human Invaders in Elfland*. It was good, better than the other two. I've started reading some of my older ones all over again. I've only got one left that I haven't read. I'm saving it for Sunday. Next week I'm going to see if I can get my mother to take me downtown to the city library and look for more in the series.

We all went to church that Sunday: me, Jason, Mom and Dad, just like always. If Mom didn't feel good, she didn't let on. She smiled at me when the organist started playing her favorite hymn, "Amazing Grace." I didn't join in; I just listened to Mom sing. It was wonderful. She seemed fine, and I stopped worrying about her in the back of my mind.

That was my last day of vacation. I'd been going to the same school since the first grade, so I wasn't as worried as Sharon was. I had friends I'd known for four years: Jerry Morris, Fred Locke, Alan Wydman, George Milhaus, Juan and Jose Muñoz, and Percy Hall. I knew most of the guys at school. George and Fred and I used to play at the park near home, some Saturdays.

The first day of school was great, because there wasn't a lot of class work, mostly just getting our books and being told where to sit and so on. After that, we went out and played on the schoolyard, and I got to tell all my friends about our trip to Montana and show them some of my photos.

Jerry Morris had gotten a ton of new computer games that summer. He and I made a deal to swap three of my old ones for three that he was tired of: I swapped *Revenge of the Mechozoids, Dungeon Fortress of Flufelberg,* and *Submarine War XI: Run Silent But Deadly* for his *Tofu Tycoon, Arena of Blood–Type O,* and *Perils of GI George VII: R&R.* That was very cool.

That was a good day for me. Sharon's first day at school was not nearly as good as mine.

September 13: Dear Millicent, well, school was bad enough, today. It could have been worse, I suppose. A lot of people had icky-colored jeans on. By people, of course, I mean girls. The boys, who are not people, were mostly dressed up like total dorks. Some even had pants that didn't fit or that were torn and dirty. They looked really, really stupid. Not that I should talk; nobody else had crappy shoes like mine, except one goofy boy, and his were brown, not orangey-red. With my shoes and my hair, I look hideous.

I'm sure nobody named Millicent ever had cheesy home haircuts or wore waffle-stompers. I couldn't do much about the haircut, but I took the shoes off and hid them in my backpack right after school. I thought about chucking the damn things in the trash can and telling Mother I'd lost them. Do you think that would work, Mill? Neither do I.

The emergency "ersh" bar remnant didn't last past early morning recess. I went up to a group of the girls and tried to talk with them, but they pretty much just ignored me and went on with their conversation. I guess I didn't have anything much to say, anyway. I was so bummed, I ate the whole ersh bar. I'd been hoping it would last 'til lunch.

I have six classes: Social Studies and Phys. Ed., then recess. Right after that comes English. After lunch there's Math, Science and Art. I get out at 3:30. Mother picked me up at 3:45. Last year at Columbus, I had to wait for her until 4:00. The Tech-a-Temp people here have her working part time at Webb & Company, so she gets off a little earlier. That means I should get picked up earlier, too, but Mother has a hard time tearing herself away from her job, no matter what it is. Oh, well, if she's late, I can always do more homework or study. The benefits go on and on.

There's this boy in my grade. He's tall and cute. He has brown hair and nice eyes. I think they're sort of green. His last name is Greene, too. Not that I'm boy-crazy, Mill. Mostly I think they're a bunch of monkeys. But if I were boy-crazy, I'd like David. He wears good clothes and smiles a lot and says funny things. I wonder how I can get to know him better.

CHAPTER 3
MOM IS LATE

A couple of weeks had gone by since that time in the backyard when something happened to Mom. I'd totally forgotten about it. As far as I knew, everything was okay this day. It was Thursday, still the first week of school. I had my new basketball and was shooting baskets in the schoolyard while I waited for Mom to pick me up. Her red SUV used to pull up to the side gate every day right at 3:40. That gave me a few minutes to practice my shots.

After a while, I felt like I'd been tossing the ball at the hoop for a really long time. I looked at my watch, and it was 3:50. She was late. I looked up and down the street and didn't see her coming. I started to get antsy. I practiced some more, but my heart wasn't in it. She'd never been this late before, except the time the battery died in her old car.

By then, I was all by myself on the schoolyard. Jerry and Fred had hung out for a few minutes and then they went home. All the teachers' cars were gone. Mr. Gardner, the custodian, was still around. The only other kid left was a girl sitting under the stairs, studying. She'd stuffed her shoes and socks into the top of her backpack and was leaning against the wall with a book in her lap.

She was new in our school. She was the smallest in our class. When I first saw her, I thought she was a 4th grader. She was real quiet in class, but always knew the answers when the teacher called

11

on her. I hadn't thought about it much, but I had noticed she was sort of cute. Dark hair, cut short, with bangs. I tried to remember her name—Cheryl or Sherrie or something like that.

It was getting very late. To stop worrying, I decided to see how many baskets I could sink in a row. The most I got up to was three. I couldn't focus on what I was doing and kept hitting the rim. After four o'clock, I stopped shooting and leaned against the pole and just watched the street, looking for Mom's car. I started wondering more and more where she was. By now, I was thinking a lot about that time in the backyard.

After a while, the girl came over and said, "Is your mother late?"

"Uh, yeah." I bounced the ball a couple of times. I was rattled and I guess it showed.

"My mother is always late," she said.

"My mom is never late. Just once, last year." I took a shot. Missed.

"Don't worry. Maybe her car wouldn't start, or something."

But Mom's car was new and always started okay, so I went right on worrying. I got the ball and tried again and missed. The girl caught it on one hand on the rebound and tossed it to me, all in one motion. Smooth.

She put down her backpack, and we took turns shooting at the hoop. I wanted to impress her, I guess, but she was accurate and I was nervous, so she sank way more baskets than I did. I tried harder, but still didn't do so great. So much for looking like a hot-shot basketball star. I was so bad, I had to say something. I thought up a couple of feeble excuses, but finally just said, "You're not bad," instead. She grinned. I liked that.

We kept shooting. About twenty after four, my dad showed up. He'd already parked and come to the basketball court before I saw him. He didn't smile or anything like he usually does. He just said, "David, your mom hasn't been feeling very good, and I had to take her to the doctor this afternoon."

Then I knew for certain that Mom had something really wrong with her. There was this long silence. I didn't know what to say. I guess I was afraid. Nobody else said anything, either. Then Dad looked at the girl, since she was standing right beside me.

I blurted out, "This is Cheryl, Dad. She's in my class."

"I'm Sharon, Mr. Greene. Sharon Quandres."

Sharon, not Cheryl. Arrgh! I felt like a moron and wanted to dig a hole and crawl into it.

"Do you need a ride, Sharon?" he said.

"Yes. My mother's late. Can you drop me off on Beech Street? Near 77th Street."

"Sure. That's just one street over from us," Dad said.

When we pulled up in front of Sharon's, I could see the back of our house, right behind her place. We were neighbors. That was cool. I watched her run inside as we pulled away. I liked the way she ran, smooth, without a lot of effort, even with her backpack.

Once we were home, Dad dropped another bomb on me. We were still in the living room, and before I could run up to my room, he said, "David, your mother is asleep upstairs. Don't disturb her. She had some tests earlier this week, and the doctor told us today that she has cancer."

I felt my stomach drop inside me. "Cancer?" was all I could say. I was flattened.

Dad held up a hand. "She's going to have some surgery in a few days, and then she'll have to have treatments for several months."

I kept thinking, this only happens to people on TV; this couldn't happen to my mom. "She's going to get better, isn't she?"

"Yes. The doctor says she's got an excellent chance of a full recovery."

He said "excellent." I ignored the "chance" part and stopped worrying. She was going to be okay. I took a deep breath.

"I'll have to take your mom to the hospital and to her treatments and doctor visits," he said. "And I still have to go to work every day. You'll have to help me and your mother by doing more chores around the house. You'll have to look after Jason, too."

I was okay with all of that. At least, I thought so. How could I not be? Mom was sick, and I thought if I did everything Dad asked, it would help. Then Mom would be all right. It sure didn't take long for me to mess up in the Jason department.

Dad went to Grandma Greene's to pick up Jason. I tiptoed up to my room so I wouldn't wake Mom, and started my homework. I had a hard time concentrating, so I played Mind-Sweeper on my computer for a while to relax. It's real easy; you just find all the mines without blowing any up. I felt better almost right away, but I kept on playing until Dad and Jason got back.

Later, while Dad and I were fixing something quick for dinner, he said, "Take Jason upstairs and get him ready for bed. And don't wake your mother up."

I managed to get Jason up to our room without making a sound. But he didn't want to get ready for bed that early, and I couldn't get him all the way into his jammies. He pulled away from me and started down the hall to the big bedroom. I was afraid he'd wake up Mom, so I grabbed him. He twisted around and tried to get away from me, then fell down and landed on his butt. He cried and yelled, even though he wasn't hurt all that much.

Dad came upstairs. "What the hell are you doing?" he said, sort of yelling and whispering at the same time. "Do you call this helping? You're supposed to get Jason ready for bed, not make a ruckus."

He'd never talked to me like that before. I already felt bad; now I felt awful. "It was Jason's fault—"

"You're older than he is. You should be able to handle a simple task."

I never got a chance to tell him my side of it. By then, Mom was up. That made Dad even madder at me. He tried to talk Mom into going back to bed, but she was already awake. She took care of Jason, and I could tell that Dad was still angry later, at dinner. He didn't look at me, and he was real nice to Jason. I wanted to kick the little turd.

After dinner, Dad went upstairs with Mom and Jason, so I sat in the den and watched TV for longer than usual. I totally forgot to do my Social Studies homework. It was a bad day, the worst I could remember.

But, in one way, it had been a good day, too, because it was the day I met Sharon. It was the first time I talked to her.

It was special for Sharon, too, I found out later.

September 16: Dear Millicent, I talked with David today, after school! He was waiting for his mother to pick him up. We played with his basketball while we waited. He told me I was good at shooting baskets! Actually, Mill, what he said was, "not bad." I'm pretty sure that means "good" in boy-speak. Then his father came and gave me a ride home. My mother worked late and asked my father to pick me up. He forgot, of course. But I'd rather ride home with David, so I'm glad he forgot.

I'm getting desperate for some better clothes. I've squeezed into a couple more outfits from last year. I know I look like a freak. I met two girls who will talk to me, but they dress a little funny, too. They're okay, though. Their names are Betty Lou and Mary Jane. It's better than not knowing anybody at all. I told them I'm from California. They asked if I ever saw any movie stars, so I made up a bunch of stories, like seeing Dustin on Hollywood Blvd. and Harrison in Studio City, as if we call them by their first names there. I named some other stars I'd "seen." I guess I should have written them down so I don't get my stories mixed up. I sure hope they don't find out I was only four when we lived in California!

I finished reading my last Elfin-Trek book. I sort of miss that feeling of having one left I haven't read. They don't have any Elfin-Treks in the school library. They've got the complete Bobbsey Twins but no Elfin-Trek, would you believe it? Barf! They had Lord of the Rings, but somebody stole the second book. I guess it doesn't matter, since I've already read them and The Hobbit, but it shows how crummy the school library is. I guess they don't get enough money to buy any good books.

CHAPTER 4
COPING

The next morning was not too bad. When I went downstairs, Mom was in the kitchen, fixing breakfast like she always did. I felt relieved. Dad had told me she was going to be all right, and she seemed okay. I tried hard to keep Jason from bothering her. Then I remembered I had Social Studies stuff to do, so I had to stop watching Jason and try to get the homework done on the kitchen table.

Of course, while I was working on the homework, Jason got up and ran around and knocked his orange juice off the table. I got down and started to soak the juice up with my napkin. Jason stood there and cried. I was really mad at him.

Mom put her hand on my shoulder. "I'll get it, David. You just finish your homework. Jason, sit down and eat your cereal."

Then Dad came in and saw Mom down on her knees cleaning up the floor. "Now what?" he said, looking at me and Jason.

"It's nothing," Mom said. "Jason just knocked over his juice."

"David, you're supposed to be helping your mother!"

"I know—"

Mom jumped in and tried to get me off the hook. "Don, I told David to finish his homework. I can take care of the floor."

Dad looked at me. "Homework? Didn't you get it done last night?"

I thought he wasn't being fair, so I lied a little. "I got most of it done. I only have a paragraph to do."

We ate breakfast, and then Dad took me to school. I ran into Sharon in the hallway just before class started. I was glad to see her, after all that had happened. "How is your mother?" she asked.

"The doctor says she has cancer."

Sharon put her hand on my arm. "She'll be okay, won't she?"

"She'll have to have surgery and treatments and pills. My dad says she'll get better in a while."

Then I told her about Jason and the homework and everything. It made me feel better to tell her. She offered to help me get the homework done, but the bell rang and it was too late to do anything. Even so, I felt good, because I knew Sharon was my friend now.

Things started to go downhill fast after that last almost-normal morning. Mom didn't feel well in the afternoon, so Dad brought home sandwiches. The deli had put mustard on all the bread. I'm allergic to mustard, so I had to eat cereal, instead. Ack!

On Saturday morning, Mom couldn't get out of bed. Dad tried to scramble eggs for breakfast. He did the best he could, but the eggs were sort of brown on the bottom and tasted burnt. I got yelled at again, and I didn't even *do* anything. I knew it wasn't fair. Dad never used to yell at me. I wanted to get away, so I took Jason over to the park and we played for hours. I forgot about everything for a while.

This was about the time when Sharon started having strange dreams.

September 20: Dear Millicent, last night, I had a bizarre dream about my old doll, Emily. I still have Emily, but I haven't played with her for years. I keep her in my dresser drawer. In the dream, she's alive and makes sounds and everything, just like a real baby. Weird. I think I've had that same dream before, maybe a dozen times.

I saw David again. He looked worried, and he didn't smile at all. His mom has cancer. I hope she doesn't die, or something. If my mother died, it would be ultra-dreadful.

Living with just my father would be beyond awful. I'd *really* have to run away!

School stinks. There's this blonde girl at school who thinks she's totally hot. I guess all the other girls think so, too—most of them, anyway. They hang around her like she's the queen, or something. She is pretty, but a little chubby. Her name is Rowena Broadburn. I said 'hi' to her today, just to see what would happen. She didn't say anything, but she did smile at me. That's a start.

Wednesday, the evening before her operation, Mom got ready to go to the hospital. She put on her old blue dress with white flowers on it. It was once her favorite dress to wear to church, but she'd lost weight and it didn't fit right. I helped her get down the little black suitcase, the one she took to Montana. She packed it with a few things, and then we went downstairs and waited in the living room for Dad and Jason to get home.

I guess I looked worried. Mom put an arm around me and said, "Don't worry, David; I'll be fine. Dr. Roedling is a good surgeon, so I'm in the best hands possible."

"When will you be home again?"

"Just a few days. You can come and see me tomorrow night. Everything will be okay."

I just held onto her hand and prayed in my head. *God, please make Mom okay.*

Dad came home with Jason, and then we took Mom to the hospital. I waited in the car with Jason, looking up at the big brick building and wondering which window would be her room. When Dad came back, he said the operation would take two or three hours Thursday morning, and that we could go see her Thursday night or maybe Friday.

Dad took all day Thursday off from work so he could be at the hospital while Mom was having her surgery. I got the day off from school, too. Dad wanted me to wait at home with Grandma Greene and Jason, but I begged until he let me go with him. He made me bring along my school books and do homework while we waited.

Hospitals smell bad. They're boring, too. Nothing to do in the waiting room, unless you like yucky daytime TV—soap operas and crap. The magazines were a year old and had half the covers torn off. Homework was more interesting, but I didn't get much done, as it turned out.

The seating was old, shiny metal tube chairs, with new plastic covers. Dad and I were the only ones in the waiting room that morning. They let him know when she went in to the operating room, which was on the other side of some double doors with big, round windows in them. We didn't talk much. Mostly we just sat there. I tried to study, but couldn't, so I worried instead.

I thought we'd be there until 10 o'clock, at least, but it was only an hour before a guy came through the doors wearing what looked like green pajamas and a dorky hat. He was peeling off rubber gloves. "Mr. Greene?" he said to my dad.

Dad stood up. "Yes?"

"I'm Doctor Roedling. We've done everything we can at this stage . . . " He stopped and looked at me for a second. "Is this your boy?"

My dad said, "Yes. This is David."

"How are you, David?" the doctor said. He didn't wait for an answer, but talked to my dad again. "Why don't we leave your boy here for a minute, and I'll give you some information on post-op care, and so on. Step this way." He looked at me again and said, "We'll be right back, David."

They went through the double doors and left me there for a long time. I got up and walked around the room, then sat down on one of the chairs. I picked up my Social Studies book and just flipped through it. I was glad the operation part was over so fast. I knew they'd get done early if they didn't find much cancer in my mom.

After a long time, Dad finally came back out and sat down. He was holding a bunch of pamphlets and papers the doctor had given him. He looked tired. I was tired too, though it was still early. A nurse brought Dad some water in a paper cup and then disappeared back through the double doors.

"How is Mom?" I asked him.

He looked at me. "She's fine, David. She'll be okay. She's just going to need a little more treatment than they thought. I'll come back later today and talk to her when she wakes up."

I got a little nervous after that, but Dad said, "Don't worry. She's getting the best care. She'll be fine. We'll both come back and see her tomorrow afternoon." He smiled at me.

Dad made me go to school the next day. He said he had a lot of things to do, and it was easier if I didn't stay home. I didn't think so, but he's the boss. At least I got to see Sharon. She was unhappy because she didn't feel like she fit in. Most of the girls ignored her, and, well, I was busy with my friends most of the time at lunch and recess. I felt a little guilty about that and wish I'd taken time to talk with her a lot more.

Dad took me back to the hospital to see Mom right after school. Jason was still at Grandma's. When we went into the room, Mom was lying flat in a bed with railings on the sides so she couldn't fall out. She had a lot of tubes fastened to her. Her eyes were only half open, and she sounded funny when she talked. I felt sad to see her like that, and my stomach sort of ached.

She took my hand and gave it a squeeze. "Hi, David." Dad sat and held her other hand.

"Are you okay?" I asked.

"Yes, I'm better than yesterday, anyway. I'll be home in a few days. Don't worry. Give Jason a hug for me."

Dad talked with Mom a while, and then she seemed tired, so he took me home.

The next few days were weird, with Mom being away and all. Once or twice, I wondered, *What if it stayed like this? What if Mom doesn't come home?* I pushed that thought right out of my head.

CHAPTER 5
MOM RETURNS

I didn't really think about Sharon for a while, because there was too much going on at home. We didn't see each other a lot until the day Dad brought Mom home, September 30th.

I was sure glad to see Mom. Jason and me were waiting for her in the living room. Dad pulled the car into the driveway, and we went outside to see her while he helped her inside. Jason was going nuts, jumping around and getting in the way. Mom wasn't well enough to hug us, so she patted us on the head, and Dad took her up to their bedroom. I felt a lot better, knowing she was home in bed, resting.

September 30: Dear Millicent, Queen Rowena Broadburn finally deigned to speak to me today. She was in the hallway with a bunch of her toady friends all clustered around her. As I walked past, she called out, "Nice shoes, Sharon!" Then she covered her mouth and rolled her eyes and giggled. All the other girls laughed, too. I felt like dirt, Mill. I've got to get rid of these shoes.

The day wasn't all bad. After school, I got to see the inside of David's house. It has two stories, with all the bedrooms upstairs, and it's nice, Mill—no stacks of junk all over the place, no holes in the carpet. Everything is neat and clean, and so is the yard. No weeds!

David's mother was just home from the hospital. She's been pretty sick. She sat up for a minute to say hello to us when we went upstairs. She's really sweet. David is lucky to have two nice parents. I hope she gets better soon.

David has his own computer. That is so great! His room is messier than mine, but not bad for a boy, I suppose. Maybe it's cluttered because David has to share the room with his little brother, Jason. Jason is cute. David calls him a twerp, but he likes him a lot, though he pretends he doesn't. I saw him give Jason a hug when he thought I wasn't looking.

October 1: I think I'm getting too big for my waffle-stompers, and they aren't very stretchy because of the heavy soles. I've had to take the laces out so my feet don't get killed. I go barefoot after school. I told Betty Lou and Mary Jane that all the kids at my school in California wear their shoes without the laces or go barefoot because we're so close to the beach. Some people will believe anything, Milli!

I only remember going to the beach once, Milli. It was a warm, sunny day. I was really little. My father took me down to where the waves hit the beach and held me up above the water when I got scared. My mother brought a picnic lunch. I found a little heart-shaped rock that I brought home with me. It was the nicest day I can remember from California.

October 2: At last, Mother had time to take me to the big library. I've been hinting for weeks that we should go there. Finally, I used my Bambi eyes on her. That always works. Well, almost always.

The librarian is nice. Her name is Ms. Nakagawa. She helped me find a bunch of Elfin-Trek books that I haven't read yet. I checked out two of the earliest ones, and two Ray Bradbury books. They're science fiction.

October 3: Dear Millicent, I finished reading both the Elfin-Trek books. They were super! I've started the first Ray Bradbury book, *Golden Apples of the Sun*. He wrote it a long time ago, but it's still good.

Sunday, when we got home from church, Mom got up for a few minutes and had lunch with us downstairs in the kitchen. Then Dad helped her back up to her room.

Later, Sharon came over and showed me the science fiction book she was reading, and I read a little bit of it. "It's fantastic!" I said.

"I'd rather read than watch TV."

"My dad doesn't let me watch TV much. He calls it the "B.R."

"B.R.?"

"Brain-rotter."

Sharon laughed. I liked hearing her laugh.

"I get to watch TV a little, mostly on weekends." I added, "Or if my dad's not around."

"My father watches TV all day. He's been sick and can't work."

"That must be rough."

"Yes. We don't have a lot of money right now. That's why I'm dressed all weird."

"Weird?" I was mystified.

She pointed at her feet. She was wearing orangey shoes with heavy lug soles—like hiking boots.

They looked fine to me. "Cool. They look like combat boots."

"That's the problem! They're hideous!" she said, almost yelling. That made me nervous.

"Uh, if you say so. I don't see anything wrong with them."

"Of course you wouldn't. You're a boy." Then she smiled.

I shrugged. "Can't you get some tennies?"

"These were cheaper. My father thought it would be easier to find work here, but it's not. My mother got a job at a temp agency, and he's still looking. When he feels okay."

I was sorry to hear Sharon's dad had been sick. I knew what that was like. Mom was up and down. Some days she'd feel almost okay; other days she'd have to stay in bed. I felt especially bad those days.

When I got home from school, I'd bring in the mail and the newspaper and then take Jason out in the backyard, and we'd play with the basketball until he was worn out. If Mom was trying to sleep, I'd take him over to the park and let him chase me until he ran out of steam.

One day, Jason found a shiny piece of green glass beside the trash can near the swings. He picked it up and started playing with it. I told him to put it in the can, but he wouldn't, so I tried to take it away from him. Well, he grabbed onto it real tight, and it cut into his hand a little. Then he let go and screamed and cried. I guess it did hurt. I took him home and, of course, it was like it was all my fault that he got hurt. Dad didn't actually yell at me, but he was pretty harsh. It totally wasn't fair.

I told Sharon about what happened to Jason. She didn't seem to know what it's like to have a little brother. She said whenever something was bothering her, she'd get a book and read about elves and forget everything for a while. Sharon was really into books.

October 7: Dear Millicent, I finished Golden Apples of the Sun. I loved it. It's about strange people and places. It's so different from my world, it takes me somewhere I feel free. I want to write like that when I'm grown up, seeing the world in another way.

Betty Lou and Mary Jane and I hang out by ourselves a lot. We don't seem to fit in with the other girls. The three of us agree that Queen Rowena is a total snot. I guess that makes us a club. Ha-ha!

October 11: Dear Mill, I've got a book report to do. I finished reading the other Bradbury book, The Illustrated Man, so I'm all set. Some of the stories in there are so weird! Still, it takes me away from my humdrum life, so it's good weird.

After a few weeks, I sort of got used to Mom being sick. That doesn't sound right, but that's almost the way it was. I learned when to go in and see her and when to let her sleep. Four times a day, she was supposed to get some pills and a glass of water. If she wasn't feeling good, I'd bring her dinner up on a tray. She didn't have much appetite, though.

Mom had to go to the hospital for her treatments every few days. She was even sicker after them. I thought they were supposed to make her feel better, but they actually made her worse. I felt terrible.

Dad was real busy every morning, so he bought me my own alarm clock. I'd get up on my own and dress, then get Jason up and ready to go to Grandma's. I fixed cereal for Jason and me, too. Dad just had coffee. I guess he didn't like Sugarola Oat Lumps.

After breakfast, Dad would drive me to school. On the way, we'd drop Jason off at Grandma's place. Mom wasn't well enough to watch him, and she needed to nap a lot.

Our routine kept changing. Some days, Dad would go to work early, and Grandma would take me to school. Or she'd pick me up after school when Dad took Mom to the doctor or worked late.

At first, we'd leave Mom home on Sundays. Grandma or one of Mom's friends would stay with her while Dad and me and Jason went to church. After a while, we just went every other Sunday.

Besides looking after Jason, I had to wash the cars or do the yard work on weekends and some other chores, like doing the wash and running the vacuum. It wasn't hard, but it wasn't much fun, either. Especially the looking after Jason part. I didn't mind, because I knew things would settle down again as soon as Mom got well.

Another sad thing was that Mom's hair fell out from her treatments. She started wearing a hat, which she never did before unless it was raining or snowing. I saw her once or twice without the hat and it scared me to see her bald head. She tried not to let that happen again. I felt bad that she'd seen me looking at her. She told me it would grow back—another thing to look forward to.

CHAPTER 6
SLEEPWALKING

We were pretty well into the school year when Sharon told me she'd been sleep-walking.

October 15: Dear Millicent, I woke up last night and was kneeling in front of my dresser. I'd been walking in my sleep, I think. I'd gotten out of bed and opened the drawer where I keep Emily. I don't play with her any more like I used to, but I keep her tucked into the bottom drawer with her blanket around her, so she'll be warm and safe. Silly, huh?

I guess I was checking to see if she was okay. Isn't that weird? I put her away again, so Mother wouldn't think I'd been playing with her. As I got back into bed, I could remember doing that before, maybe almost every night. It's like a dream that goes away if you don't remember it first thing in the morning. I wonder why I do it. She's just a doll.

October 16: Dear Millicent, we took the books back to the library this afternoon. I got four more Elfin-Treks and three sci-fi books. On the way back, we stopped at a grubby thrift shop and got some more cheap clothes for me to wear to school. They weren't worn very much—no gaping holes, at least—but I wasn't exactly excited about them, and I guess it showed. Mother kept telling me "They fit you really well." Which is true, but I'm still ticked off, Mill. I'm the only girl in the whole school that wears thrift shop clothes.

October 17: Dear Millicent, **he** was drunk again last night. He and Mother were yelling real late. He broke something in their room, smashed it against the wall. I think from the crunch it made that it was the clock radio. Again. Oh, well, it's not like he needs it. He doesn't get up till noon because he still doesn't have a job. I hate it here. I want to run away.

October 18: Dear Millicent, I got tired of telling Betty Lou and Mary Jane stories about movie stars I'd seen. I don't like lying to my friends, and it was getting hard to keep my stories straight, so I told them I'd left California a long time ago. They promised they wouldn't tell anybody.

Mother forgot to pick me up at school today. Again. She told me later she was very busy and just forgot about the time. I bummed a ride home with David and his father. David's father is really nice, not like mine.

Mother finally remembered she was supposed to pick me up (as if she hasn't done this every school day for years!). By the time she got to the school, I was already on the way home with David. She went ape, thought I'd been kidnapped by gypsies or something. (I wish! It would be an improvement over living with **him**. Maybe I could learn to play the violin.) When she finally thought to call home and found out I was already there, she got mad at me. She yelled and screamed over the phone. She makes everything seem like it's my fault. I'm not the one who forgot to pick me up. It just isn't fair.

Grandma would watch Jason during the day, usually at her place. Dad still had to take Mom to the hospital or the doctor and do all the shopping and errands she used to do. He had to bring work home to make up for the time he spent taking care of Mom. After dinner, he'd turn on his computer in the den and work till midnight or later. I didn't get a chance to talk to him about things like I used to. It bothered me. I wanted Mom to get better, like *now*.

Most nights, I didn't sleep real well. I'd lie there and pray that Mom would get better. Then I'd worry. When I slept, a lot of times I dreamt that Mom and I had gone somewhere, and she went away and I couldn't find her. The next day, I'd drag around and be half asleep in class, or staggering like a zombie in P.E. The next night, I'd fall asleep before I got my homework done. I'd try to get up early and do my work, but sometimes it was just too hard to get out of bed.

After school, Dad couldn't pick me up until after four o'clock, which was fine with me. Sharon was always there, waiting for her mother. After George and the rest of the guys left, she'd come and talk to me. Then, if her mom hadn't shown up yet, when Dad got there, he'd give Sharon a ride home. I liked that, too. Dad was real nice to her, and he'd talk to her instead of asking me his usual questions about how was I doing in school. I didn't like being asked.

Sharon and I swapped phone numbers so she could call if she needed a ride to school. And so we could just talk, if we wanted to.

I was doing okay in school. Almost okay. My teacher sent home a progress report, but Dad was too busy to read it. He just signed the brown envelope it comes in and gave it to me to take back to school. I peeked at the report. It said I wasn't doing as good in Social Studies and English as I had before. Not too bad, with all that was going on.

But even though there was a lot going on in Sharon's life, too, she still got good grades. Otherwise, school was the pits for her.

October 26: Dear Millicent, this is maybe the worst day of my life. Queen Rowena gave me another treat for lunch. She waited until I was nearby, and then she told all her kissy friends that I wasn't really from California, that I hadn't lived there for a long time. I was going to call her a liar, but then I saw Betty Lou standing there, smiling and acting like she was part of Rowena's bunch. She must have told Rowena what I'd said. What a little rat! I feel awful. I have no friends, Mill, except David. And you. And Mary Jane.

October 27: I get a ride home from David's dad every day now. Mother is too busy with work to pick me up, even though she wouldn't admit it. She gets so wrapped up in work, she forgets everything else. Including me. I guess she forgets my father, too. That's a definite plus. I asked her if I can just ride home with David from now on. She got all mothery and went, "Who are these people? Are they safe?" and stuff like that. Like all of a sudden it matters? They've been taking me home for weeks. I told her they live right behind us, in the yellow house. She went and met David's father for two minutes, and then said it's okay for me to ride home with David.

October 29: Dear Millicent, more shouting last night. My father was drunk when I got home. He was reeling around in the living room, trying to sing. He smelled like he'd been gargling turpentine. I absolutely hate him. He can't be my real father. I'd be totally ashamed to be related to somebody like him. He must really be my stepfather. If he was my real father, he wouldn't yell and scream at me the way he does.

I'd better hide you in a super safe place, Millicent. If he found you and read what I think about him, I'd be history.

October 30: Dear Millicent, school is about the same. At least Mary Jane hasn't gone over to the enemy. She and I spent recess yesterday listing wonderful ways to get even with Rowena and Betty Lou. None of which will happen, Mill. They just aren't worth it. It's fun to think about, though.

I finally met Sharon's mom when she came to get Sharon at our house after school. Mrs. Quandres seemed okay, but was in a big hurry to get home. Sharon looks a lot like her, but is calmer, and smiles more. Sharon has pretty brown eyes like my mom, too.

CHAPTER 7
SAILING

M rs. Whitworth was our homeroom teacher and taught English, too. One day she read us a poem.

The Silver Dream

Come sail away on my silver dream,
Cast off the hawsers of care;
Leave all your troubles and sail away
Over the ocean with me.
Come sail away on my silver dream,
Let the wind blow through your hair.
Feel the sun and the salt water spray,
Know what it means to be free.
Come sail away on my silver dream,
Breathe in the fresh, briny air.
Let your heart soar on the wind today,
Over the sapphire sea.

Sharon and I talked about the poem at my house after school. "What are hawsers?" I asked.

"Big ropes that tie the boat to the dock."

"I liked that poem."

Sharon sighed and said, "Me too. It makes me want to get a boat and just sail away and never come back."

I didn't like the idea that she would leave. I knew she wasn't serious, but it still bothered me. "Not ever?" I said.

"You can come, too."

That was better. A lot better. "Thanks. But where would we go?"

"Lots of places," she said. "Places like Bora Bora and Rangoon."

"Those sound pretty strange."

"They probably are. We should go to Pago Pago, too."

"How 'bout Walla Walla?"

She laughed. "I don't think you can get there on a boat."

"Timbuktoo?"

She shook her head, making her hair sway back and forth. "No water there, either."

"Timbukthree?"

She smiled. "That sounds dry, too. Try another place."

"Well, I've always wanted to see Lake Titicaca. There's got to be water there."

She laughed again. "Yes, but it's surrounded by mountains. You'd have to bring the boat in on a truck. Maybe we could go to Hong Kong."

"That sounds cool."

Sharon wrote the *Silver Dream* poem down, and I made copies for both of us on my computer.

Later, I asked my dad how hard it was to build a boat. He said it was very hard, and told me about some guy who built a boat in his basement and then couldn't get it out the door.

I knew it really wasn't practical to get a boat and go away. Even if I was old enough, Mom and Dad wouldn't like it. And I supposed Jason would miss me.

But Sharon was still thinking a *lot* about sailing away.

November 3: Dear Millicent, we had poetry yesterday in English. David made me a copy of the poem we studied, and I taped it to the back of my door. I always keep my room neat and clean, so my mother never comes in here, and she doesn't see that side of my door. I've got pictures there that I don't show anybody else, like my unicorns and elves, and a few poems.

I'd like to have a boat and call it the "*Silver Dream*," just like in the poem, and sail off to exotic places. With David for company. I wonder how much a boat would cost.

November 5: Dear Millicent, I found pictures of a sailing ship just like the one I want some day. It's beautiful, with mahogany decks and brass fittings and white sails. I showed the best picture to David and then taped it to my door.

One day early in November, Mom was downstairs when I got home from school.

"You're up!" I said.

She smiled. "Yes, I think I'm getting better. It's been weeks since the surgery. I need to get up for a little bit every day now."

I gave her a big hug, the first in a long time. I guessed the medicine had finally started to take effect. I stopped feeling so tense.

Sharon and I talked with Mom and Grandma in the kitchen for a while. It made me happy to see them all together. Sharon told Mom about "our boat" and showed us a picture she'd found in a magazine of a big sailboat.

"It's a lovely boat, Sharon," Mom said. "I hope you own one someday. Now, I think I'll go up and rest. It's been good to see you." She touched Sharon's shoulder and then went upstairs with Grandma.

Sharon sat and talked some more. "This is the bow and this is the stern," she said, pointing at the front and back ends of the boat.

"Uh, I knew that."

"Okay, Mr. Know-it-all, what's this?" she asked, pointing at the pole in the middle of the boat.

"Easy. That's the mast."

"And this down here?"

"The bottom?"

"That's the keel," she told me.

"What's this?" I pointed at a rope thingie.

"That's a halyard. They put flags and pennants on it."

"How about this thing on the deck?"

"That's a binnacle."

"I thought a binnacle was a little cone-shaped critter on the bottom . . . I mean, the keel." I didn't really think that, but I wanted to hear her laugh.

She did laugh and then said, "That's a barnacle, you silly twerp!"

Some days after school, we'd draw pictures of the *Silver Dream*, or talk about where we could go in it. In *her*. Boats are always called "*her*." Sharon told me that. We weren't planning to actually go out and buy a boat, but it was fun to just talk about. And it was better than thinking about what was going on at home.

Sharon needed something to take her mind off what was happening at her house, too.

November 12: Dear Millicent, I heard them yelling in the bedroom again last night. They were shouting things at each other, and then **wham!** I guess Mother fell down. She went out into the living room and started crying. She seemed okay at breakfast, so I guess she wasn't really hurt. Millicent, I need some more fantasy books to take me away.

CHAPTER 8
ROUGH SEAS

My mom had started to get better early in November. One day, about the middle of the month, Sharon and I got home, and Mom wasn't downstairs to greet us. I ran upstairs to see if she was okay. She was sitting up on the bed.

"Hi, David," she said.

"Aren't you going to come downstairs?"

"I'm just a little tired today. I'll be down tomorrow when you get home. Now, give me a hug, and I'll lie down for a while." I was a little worried, but I hugged her and went downstairs to get a snack with Sharon.

I guess Sharon could see I was worried. She asked how Mom was, and I told her. It bothered me a lot that Mom hadn't felt able to come and talk with Sharon and me.

The next day, Mom did come downstairs again. I felt a lot better, seeing her up and around.

But after that, she started getting out of bed less and less.

She cried a little, once, when Jason wasn't there to see. I put my arm around her. "Are you going to be okay?" I asked. I was really worried and my stomach felt queasy.

"Yes, I think I'm getting better. I'm just having some ups and downs, lately. I'll be fine."

I went to my room to let Mom take a nap. Later, I didn't get much chance to talk with Dad about her. He was either working or looking after Mom or worrying in the den.

One night, he took me along to a drugstore at the mall to get one of her medicines. While he was waiting, I did some early Christmas shopping. I picked out a small, white teddy bear for Jason. Then I saw a little silver angel pin with a tiny ruby in it on the early Christmas sale table. It cost more than I'd planned to spend, but it seemed perfect for Mom, somehow. I borrowed money from Dad to buy it.

It got harder and harder for Dad to work and take care of Mom and shop and cook and so on. Dad didn't want Mom to go to a nursing home; he thought she'd rest better at our place. I'm not sure she did. But if she went to the nursing home, we wouldn't be able to see her as much. At home, we could go in when she was feeling not too bad, and she'd talk to Jason and me.

Dad was pretty busy and tired, I guess. By then, we'd stopped going to church on Sundays.

He'd get really mad at me whenever I didn't remember to do all my chores. I kept forgetting stuff. He finally got an agency to send a lady to help out. Her name was Becky Tandoc. Becky was super. She took care of some cleaning, but mostly made breakfast and lunch for Mom and helped her take a shower. Then Becky would fix dinner for all of us and leave it in the fridge. All we had to do was nuke it at dinnertime. I ended up being in charge of heating stuff up. That was easy.

Homework was not. For some reason, I didn't feel like studying or doing my homework, even when it was easy stuff. I kept putting it off until it was too late.

At school, Mrs. Whitworth came up to me a few times before class. "How is your mother doing, David?" she'd ask.

"She's pretty good today."

"And how are you doing?"

I always said, "Fine."

Then she'd lean down and say, "Why aren't you getting good grades on your English and spelling tests anymore?"

I never really had an answer. I'd just shrug.

"You need to study more, David."

I said I would. And I did try to study and do more of the English work to keep Mrs. Whitworth happy. But then I let other stuff slide a little. It was hard to get started and even harder to keep going. I'd open a book and try to read, but the words just seemed too hard to focus on. My head kept going somewhere else.

Things weren't going any better for Sharon, either.

November 18: Dear Millicent, snow today. And more good news. My stepfather took the rent money, got drunk again, and spent what was left on a motorcycle. He kept saying, "Oh, I can ride it around and look for jobs, and it's a real steal. I couldn't let it get away." There's not a whole big chance it would "get away," Mill. The thing has been sitting in somebody's garage and hasn't moved an inch for the last five years. It doesn't have a chain or a gas tank. What it's got is cobwebs! He thinks he can fix it, but if I know him, he'll work on it for a few days and then give up.

Anyway, Mother was really, really mad at him. She has to pay the rent in less than two weeks, and she won't have enough money. She wants him to sell the motorcycle and get the money back, even if he has to sell it for less than he paid for it. It's Japanese. He bought it when he was drunk, so she calls it his "Full-o-Sake," but not when he can hear her. He just yells at her when she asks where the rent money's coming from.

November 25, Thanksgiving: Dear Millicent, we had frozen turkey TV dinners today, in celebration. Very appropriate, considering how much there is to be thankful for. Sigh!

I guess I'm just feeling sorry for myself, Mill. Waah! It could be worse, I suppose. Lots worse.

David is very nervous. He chews his fingernails and fusses with his hair all the time. I'm sure it's because he's anxious about his mother. I think about how I'd feel if it was my mother, and I get weak in my knees.

At least my mother is working and healthy, and I'm okay. The weather has been good, so far, this year. I still have a friend at school, Mary Jane, who is okay, and my friend David, who is really great. And I have another new batch of books to read! Heaven. Well, not bad.

I brought in the mail from the box one day and found my report card in it. I decided to open the envelope before Dad saw it and find out how good I did. I pulled the card out of the little brown sleeve. I said a bad word. I'd slipped from all A's and B's last year, to no A's at all, not even in P.E. I got C's in Math and Social Studies. I was sort of shocked.

I didn't want Mom or Dad to see these grades. They might worry. Dad might get mad. But he hadn't seen the card come in the mail, and so I figured he probably wouldn't remember it was time for report cards. I was sure I'd get better grades as soon as Mom got well. I looked in Dad's desk and took an old letter with his signature and copied it onto the brown sleeve where he was supposed to sign. It was easy to do—his signature is just a bunch of loops and a squiggle. I hid the card in my room and turned the brown sleeve in at school the next day. Would Dad realize he should have gotten my report card that week? I was pretty sure he wouldn't. He was really busy with Mom and still working a lot.

On Thanksgiving, Grandma came over and cooked turkey and everything at our place. With cranberries. It was wonderful. We all ate downstairs in the dining room, except for Mom. Then Dad and me took a tray up to her and sat beside the bed while she ate. We talked about school, and getting ready for Christmas, and where we'd go for our next vacation. Mom laughed a couple of times, so I knew she was feeling better. She said she was tired, so we gave her her night-time pills and she lay back and went to sleep.

Uncle Vince and Aunt Sophie came over for dessert. He gave me a big smile and told me a silly joke to make me laugh. Grandma put Jason to bed, so I got to stay up and play dominoes with Aunt Sophie. It was nice, but would have been nicer if Mom had been able to eat with us downstairs.

Dad got Mom a better bed, one of the hospital kind that goes up and down. She seemed to like it. When I went past her room, if she was awake, I'd go in and see if she wanted anything. She usually had water and everything on the tray where she could reach it, but I'd get her some ice or whatever she asked for. She always smiled at me and gave me a pat on the head. She wanted to hug me, but the side rails on the new bed made it sort of hard, I guess, so she'd just squeeze my hand.

I remember thinking, *it'll sure be nice when Mom is well and can give me a real hug again.*

A nurse started coming in once a day to check on Mom. I was usually at school when she came, and so I didn't find out what her name was, but I hoped she'd help Mom get well quicker. Dad said he'd need to work extra hours to cover part of the cost of the nurse.

I went in to see Mom once, and she held onto my hand really tight and started to cry. I felt awful, but I didn't cry. I thought it would make her feel worse if I cried. I just patted her arm and went to get her some water. I felt sick and sort of numb. I staggered and almost spilled the water in the hallway when I was coming back.

Mom thanked me and touched my cheek. Then I went to my room and turned on the computer and played a game for two hours instead of doing my homework.

Around then, Sharon's family was having a lot of problems, things she never told me about at the time they happened.

December 2: Dear Millicent, Mother managed to pay the rent. She was actually a day late, but the company didn't make a big deal of it. She had the temp agency give her another part time job for a few days to cover what *he* stole from her purse. She's been real tired this whole week. I've been setting the table and getting part of dinner ready before she gets home.

Today, he came into the kitchen and yelled, "I'm hungry. When's dinner going to be ready?"

I told him, "I'll make you some potatoes."

"Well, hurry it up."

Can you believe that, Mill? He buys a crummy old motorcycle with the rent money so Mother has to work two jobs, and then he's put out because he has to wait a few minutes to stuff his face! I don't know why she puts up with him. I made him some instant mashed potatoes to shut him up. I didn't mix them right, so they weren't very good, but he didn't notice. I wanted to put the whole bowl on top of his head and smoosh them, but I didn't.

Meanwhile, the "Full-o-Sake" is sitting in the garage with pieces strewn all over the floor. It turns out that there's a lot more wrong with it than a missing chain. It needs other little things, oh, like pistons, you know?

Report cards came out and I got all A's again. David was very impressed! Mother wasn't. I guess she's got other things on her mind. She used to give me a dollar for every A, but she doesn't have the money now.

CHAPTER 9
PASSAGES

I woke up on a rainy morning in early December and found my alarm clock hadn't gone off. It was almost time for school. I panicked, jumped into my clothes and yelled for Jason to get up. Then I saw his bed was empty. *At least I don't have to waste time dragging Jason out of bed,* I thought. *Maybe we can make it to school on time if I hurry; Dad can take Jason over to Grandma's in his jammies.*

As I ran to the bathroom, I looked into the big bedroom. Mom's bed was empty! I thought, *she must be feeling better and has gone downstairs.* I ran down to the kitchen to see if I could give her a hug while she was standing up.

Dad was in the kitchen, sitting at the table by the telephone. I asked, "Where's Mom?" He didn't seem to hear me. Then I thought maybe he'd had to take her back to the hospital during the night. That would be bad. I got scared. I asked again, "Dad? Where's Mom?"

He looked at me. "David, your mother passed away last night. It was very sudden." Then he put his head down and started to cry. I didn't know what to do. I felt like crying, too, but I thought that might make both of us feel worse. I tried to think of something to say that would make him feel better, but there wasn't anything that would help. Finally, I tried not to feel anything at all, just put my arm around him, like he used to do when I was little.

I stood there beside him, trying not to cry and wondering what we'd do without Mom. I couldn't imagine her not being with us. I'd thought she was going to get well. Dad had said she would, but now she was gone. It was like a giant hole had opened up in the world.

The phone rang about a minute later. Dad blew his nose and answered it. It was somebody from his office. He told them he would be back to work the next week. He said something about "arrangements." I figured he meant planning a funeral and things like that. I went out in the living room and knelt on the sofa, watching the rain run down the window while Dad talked.

He made a lot of phone calls to tell our relatives about Mom. He'd start to cry in the middle of the call, sometimes. Other times, he'd be okay until he hung up the phone. He'd already called his mom, Grandma Greene, during the night. She had come over while I was asleep and had taken Jason back to her place. That's why his bed was empty. She also turned off my alarm clock, so it wouldn't wake me up. Maybe she thought it would be better if I didn't find out about Mom for another hour. She was right about that.

A little later, I saw my Uncle Vince pull up in his BMW. I was awfully glad to see him. Dad went out in the rain to meet him. Vince hugged Dad and walked back in with his arm around him.

Uncle Vince stopped at the living room door when he saw me sitting there. "Hi, David," he said. "Are you okay?"

I said "Yes," but I really wasn't okay.

He came in and put his hand on my shoulder. "I'm sorry about your mom, David. She was a wonderful lady, and we'll all miss her a lot."

I just nodded and didn't say anything. I thought I'd cry if I tried to talk, so I just sat there and tried not to feel anything at all. After a while, I didn't.

Dad got Mom's address book from her purse, and he and Uncle Vince went through it, calling her friends. Uncle Vince made all the calls. Dad just sat there with the little book, turning the pages, deciding who to call next and looking sort of dazed.

Mr. Soames, a neighbor, came over and knocked at the door. I let him in. He said he'd seen the ambulance come during the night. Dad came out and told him the news. I think Mr. Soames already knew what had happened, but he said he was sorry about Mom and left. Then more people called and came by, friends and neighbors who'd heard that Mom had died.

It got pretty crowded in the kitchen. They brought a whole lot of stuff to eat, enough for several days. Uncle Vince finished making phone calls and went home. As I watched him drive off, I realized he hadn't smiled once. That was the only time I'd ever seen my Uncle Vince without his smile.

Dad had a lot of things to do. I'm not sure what they all were, but it was hard on him. I tried not to be angry with him for telling me that Mom was going to be all right when she wasn't. "She has an excellent chance," he'd said. I'd heard the *excellent*, but hadn't wanted to hear the *chance*, so I'd blocked it out.

Dad said I could skip school for the rest of the week. I didn't care one way or the other. I thought about calling Sharon, but I was too tired. I went upstairs and took a nap instead.

Sharon missed me while I was out.

December 6: Dear Millicent, David was not at school today. I think he must have caught that cold that went around last week. I hope he's back tomorrow. I miss him!

My stepfather sold the Full-o-Sake. At least, the thing isn't sitting in the garage anymore. There's just a big, oily spot where it used to be. Mother didn't ask him where it went, and she didn't ask him to give her the money he got for it. He's probably spent it already.

December 7: Dear Millicent, David's mother died yesterday! I thought he was just sick when he didn't come to school. We didn't hear about his mother until today. Mrs. Whitworth told us. Poor David! Right before Christmas, too!

The funeral was on Saturday. I had on my good slacks and shirt and my blue blazer. Dad was sitting on my left, where he could put an arm around me, and my cousin Rose was on my right, where Mom usually sat every Sunday. My two grandmas and my aunts and uncles were in the pews all around us. Everybody was there except Jason, who was too little for a funeral, and Aunt Kathy, who was taking care of Jason. And Mom.

Mom always went to church with us, except when she had a cold or something. So I kept having this feeling that, since she wasn't sitting with us, she'd be waiting for us when we got home, with her nose all red and a tissue in her hand. "Hello, David," she'd say. But of course it wasn't Sunday, and she wasn't sick at home. She was in the shiny, dark wood box right up near the altar. The coffin.

I couldn't believe it. I kept thinking, this shouldn't be happening. I looked at Rose a bunch of times, hoping that I'd been dreaming, that I'd see Mom sitting beside me, instead of my cousin.

There were flowers, even though it was December. I remember the smell of all the flowers. There were big bunches at each end of Mom's box, and a lot more up on the altar. A few small, white roses had been tied together with a ribbon and put on top of the coffin. They reminded me of all the times I'd seen Mom working on her rosebushes in our backyard, and especially that Saturday when she first felt the cancer.

It was hard for me not to cry. I tried not to think about Mom being gone. I just listened to the organ music. It was nice, I guess.

My mind was going all over the place. There were times when I felt like getting up and running away, but I knew that would be dumb. Wherever I went, Mom wouldn't be there, either. I looked at the coffin and thought about a magician we saw once on TV. He put this girl in a big, tall box and then *poof!* she was gone. He waved his wand-thingie and said some pretend magic words, and *poof!* there she was again, getting out of the box and smiling. I sat there in church and sort of imagined that the pastor was a magician, and that if he could wave a big wand and say the right words, he could make Mom come out of the box, just like the girl on TV.

43

After a minute or two or three of thinking that stupid stuff about the magician, I had to get back to what was really happening. What was real was that Mom wasn't going to come out of the box and smile. Ever. She was dead. And that's when I started to cry a little.

Dad put his arm around me, and Rose took my hand, and I tried not to cry because I didn't want to make them feel sadder than they already were. Which was awful. Dad's eyes were all puffy. Until Mom died, I thought dads never cried.

Near the end, they played Mom's favorite hymn, "Amazing Grace." It made me feel really sad. I loved hearing her sing that in church. I thought she sang better than anybody. Now, I didn't want to hear it if she couldn't sing it. I never wanted to hear that song again, and I didn't want to be there at the funeral at all. I guess, in a way, I sort of wasn't, for a while—I just stared at the flowers and zoned out. I don't remember much after that, until we were at the cemetery, getting out of the limousine.

There were flowers at the cemetery, too. It was foggy and very cold, and the wind ruffled everybody's hair as they stood around the grave. The pastor opened his book and said more prayers. When he was done, we all left Mom there and started back to our cars. I looked back as we walked away. Mom's coffin was still sitting on long pieces of wood, just above the hole in the ground. I guessed some men would come later and lower her into the hole and cover her up. That would be the end of it all. I almost cried again. I wanted to say "Goodbye, Mom," but I couldn't. Everybody would have thought I was dumb. And I'd have cried right after I said it.

Back at the limos, everyone was nice to me and Dad. Rose took me aside and hugged me and then wiped my face and combed my hair. The pastor came over and bent down and said something to me —I don't remember what. Finally, Dad and Rose and I got in the limo with Grandma Greene and the driver took us home.

I had a hard time not crying as soon as we walked into the house. The front hall was empty, and I still had this stupid feeling that Mom was going to be there. But she wasn't.

CHAPTER 10
LIFE WITHOUT MOM

Jason and Aunt Kathy were in the den, watching a movie. Jason ran out and said hi, and even though he'd been told a dozen times that Mom was in Heaven, he asked, "Where's Mommy?" and started crying. Dad made a choking noise and knelt down and hugged him. I kept my lips tight. My throat hurt from trying not to cry.

Aunt Kathy took care of Jason, and he didn't fuss very long. I felt really bad when he cried. After a few minutes, people started to come in. They brought a lot of salads and casseroles. Uncle Vince and Aunt Sophie brought a ham. Somebody took Dad upstairs to rest a while. Sophie gave Jason and me sandwiches and macaroni salad. Uncle Vince came over and took my hand and smiled at me. I felt awful, but I was so happy to see him right then, I smiled too.

It was all over. Mom wasn't sick any more. I couldn't be glad, but I felt like some things might not be quite so hard from then on. I didn't cry again for a long time.

We didn't go to church that Sunday. Our pastor came over for a while in the afternoon. He talked with us in the living room, and then we all prayed for a minute before he left. It was still early, but I went upstairs and slept as soon as he was gone.

I went to school on Monday. It was okay to be there. I was busy with class and saying hello to all my friends and stuff, and I sort of forgot about Mom being gone for a while. My friends already knew she'd died. I guess one of the teachers told them the week before. They didn't seem to know what to say, but I knew they cared. Mrs. Whitworth gave me a card that everybody signed, and George gave me a fancy card from him and his mother. That was kind of them.

Sharon met me in the hall right before class. I was totally surprised when she put her arms around me, pulled my face down, and kissed me on the cheek. I was glad there was nobody around so I didn't get all embarrassed. I still remember how much better I felt when she hugged me. She was wearing a red sweatshirt and black jeans. Her dark hair looked nice with the sweatshirt. I remember everything about that moment. We were standing in front of the old grey lockers, just past the drinking fountain, ten feet from the double doors at the end of the hallway. I guess that doesn't matter much, but now it seems really important to me, all of it.

That moment meant a lot to Sharon, too.

December 13: Dear Millicent, David is back. I saw him in the hall and didn't know quite what to say. I just reached up and put my arms around him. And I kissed him. Yes, I really did. Poor David! He's like a zombie a lot of the time and doesn't smile like he used to. This has been terrible for him.

Things are pretty quiet here since the motorcycle saga. My stepfather has been actually going out and looking for work, which is good, except that he uses the car. Mother has to drop me off at school, then take the car home and catch the bus to work, because *he's* too lazy to get up early and drop us off.

I've started hinting that I'd like some new shoes for Christmas. Nice ones.

Now that Mom was gone, we didn't have Becky to help out any more. We had to fix our own dinner and do all the cleaning and so on. We started eating a lot more frozen dinners. Urk! I was out of school for the holidays, and Jason and I would either stay with

Grandma Greene or she'd come over and stay at our place until Dad got home. He expected me to do a lot of chores. Once, I forgot to move the clothes from the washer to the dryer, and he got all upset at me the next day because he had to wear a dirty shirt to work.

Christmas didn't happen in our house. Mom was the one who really did all the Christmas stuff every year. She used to do most of the shopping, and do the decorations, and get the tree and put it up. We would all help with the tree: Dad would put up the lights, I'd hang the balls on the tree, and Jason was in charge of getting in the way and dropping things.

We didn't even get a tree, after Mom was gone.

I'd already bought Mom the bottle of perfume and the angel pin a few weeks before. I wasn't sure what to do with them. Part of me wanted to wrap them up and pretend she was going to be there Christmas day to open them.

Dad had bought her something, too, a necklace with little diamonds in it. I think it cost a lot of money. I came downstairs the day before Christmas and he was sitting at the kitchen table with the blue velvet box open in front of him. He wasn't making any noise, but he was crying. I turned around and went back upstairs as quietly as I could. Then when he couldn't hear me, I cried a little, too, thinking about how sad he was.

Jason missed Mom a lot, too. We had to keep telling him Mom was in Heaven and that she wasn't coming back. Then he'd say he wanted to go there and see her. That was hard for Dad to hear. He spent a lot of money on Jason that year. I guess he was trying to keep the little guy's mind off missing Mom.

It wasn't really Christmas without Mom. Everything we did reminded me she was gone. Dad got me three games for my computer, which was about all I wanted. He got me *Caverns of Throg the Merciless, Monster Mega-Bot Slug-Out,* and *Bastions of Doom.* All really killer games.

Dad also got me clothes and books, which was okay. I gave him some drug store cologne and a tie. Jason opened his presents and seemed happy with them. I'd got him a big plastic dinosaur set and the little white teddy bear. Dad said that was an Arctic bear, so we called him "Olaf." We didn't name the dinosaurs. Except for "Rex."

We did the usual Christmas things, but it wasn't the same. I felt like my heart was far away somewhere.

Sharon's holiday wasn't too great, either.

December 25: Dear Millicent, Christmas today. It's awful, Mill. I didn't have much money, so I got Mother some cheap imitation pearls from the Factory Super Goof Store, and some stationery, and a little fuzzy jewel box for the "pearls." I got *him* some cheap after-shave. I sure hope he doesn't drink it, Mill. (What I really wanted to give him was two big suitcases!)

Mother gave me some underwear, an orange, and a new pencil box for school. No shoes. She also got me a 99-cent world atlas and another Charlotte Sleuth, one I already had. But I didn't let her know that. I grinned until my jaws hurt, Mill. Then I came up here and cried. Sorry I got you wet.

After Christmas, Uncle Vince and Aunt Sophie came over in his Beamer. They brought me another Christmas present, *"Mal-de-mer Aero-Simulator II,"* a totally hot computer airplane game. The box said the advanced simulator mode has an actual airsickness feature. How cool is that? Uncle Vince knows what I like.

Uncle Vince drove Dad and me to the mall to get some ice cream for after dinner and to return the presents we'd bought for Mom. At the last minute, I asked if I could keep the angel pin. It seemed really important to have it, even though Mom was gone. Dad started to argue with me, but Uncle Vince said something, and Dad told me it was okay to hang onto it as long as I wanted to. I felt better then.

My aunt and uncle and my cousins came over to our place for New Year's Eve. Everybody said "Happy New Year," at midnight. I sure didn't expect the year to be very happy.

I guess Sharon felt the same way. And for good reasons.

CHAPTER II
THE NEW YEAR

J anuary 1: Dear Millicent, a new year, full of bad things just
waiting to happen. Happy New Year, Mill.

I think he hit my mother in their room again last night.
More yelling. Things breaking. She had a big bruise on her
cheek this morning. She tried to keep that side away from me,
but I saw it when I went to the sink to wash my cereal bowl.
She was very quiet, except I heard her sniff a couple of times.
He wasn't up, of course.

I didn't get enough sleep. I had that dream about Emily
again, and I woke up and couldn't go back to sleep. I finally
got up and took Emily out and held her for a minute. Then I
read a book until I felt sleepy.

A new year had started, our first without Mom. It bothered me a
lot that she wasn't going to be here for it. It didn't seem fair.

I'd been doing about the same in school. I wasn't studying much,
but some of what we were doing was real easy, and some stuff we'd
covered the year before, so my grades weren't any better, but they
weren't any worse, either. Not much, anyway. I thought maybe I'd do
better after things settled down at home.

Jason was crying a lot and having tantrums, especially when Dad was out and I was supposed to be baby-sitting. Jason missed Mom maybe more than I did. When he'd start to cry, sometimes I'd take him out to Mom's little, red SUV. We'd sit close together in the backseat and pretend to be going somewhere with Mom. He'd stop crying, make car noises for a minute or two, and then fall asleep. I'd wait there with him until Dad got back, and we'd take Jason inside and put him on the couch under a blanket.

But not long after Mom died, Dad told me he was putting an ad in the paper to sell her car.

"Can't we keep it?" I asked. I knew Jason would miss it.

Dad shook his head. "David, we don't need two cars. I don't want to pay the insurance and license fees. It would be silly to keep it."

I suppose he was right. But Jason felt really bad the day the people came and drove off in it. He didn't know what was happening at first, but when they drove it away, he had an awful tantrum, screamed and yelled, then fell down and cried. I didn't cry, or anything, though. It was just a car. Why should I cry about a car? I felt a little bad, but I think that was because Jason was so sad.

My dad had to work late, sometimes. We needed the extra money to pay the doctor bills that insurance didn't cover. Because Dad was so busy, Grandma Greene started picking Sharon and me up after school, and then we'd all go to my house.

Sharon could have gone right home then, but she'd stay at our place, and we'd have something to eat and talk until her mom got off work. Sometimes we'd watch old movies on TV, but usually we'd just talk about "our boat." She drew pictures of the *Silver Dream* in ports around the world. They were really nice. Her hands look good holding a pencil. I told her she should be an artist or a designer, like my dad. She said she wanted to be a writer. She got A's in English all the time, so I figured maybe she would.

I never went over to her house. She said it was too messy for company. It looked okay from the outside. During the summer, I'd seen her dad in the backyard, pulling weeds. He never stayed outside for long, so mostly the weeds got bigger. Then her mom would come out and mow the grass, weeds, leaves, old newspapers, everything.

I guess I should say Sharon never told me any of the stuff about her dad until a lot later. As far as I knew, everything was okay at her house. She had a mom and a dad, and she never whined. I never thought her dad might be drinking too much. I didn't even know there were people like that. She told me he was really her stepfather.

Dad hired a maid service to clean our house, but it cost a lot and didn't work out, so I started doing the cleaning again. After dinner, I'd turn on my computer. I told Dad I had English homework to do, but mostly I was just playing games. I'd plan to play for a half hour before starting my homework, but I'd get lost in what I was doing, fighting robots or stuff, and forget about everything else. I'd stop and look up and it would be ten o'clock. Then I'd have to get Jason and me ready for bed before Dad found out we were still up.

A lot of times, Jason would already be asleep on the floor. I'd have to stand him up, steer him into the bathroom, point him in the right direction, and then help him get into bed, clothes and all. In the morning, I always made sure I got Jason up before Dad came in and found him still in his clothes from the day before. I knew Dad wouldn't be too happy with that.

I liked school, but I didn't like it when the teacher asked me a question and I didn't have a clue. Sometimes I got lucky, but a lot of times the question was about homework I hadn't done. I didn't do so hot on tests, either. Otherwise, school was fine. There was something going on all the time, and I didn't think about Mom being gone, except maybe during tests when I couldn't come up with answers.

Sharon always had the right answers. At school, anyway. At Sharon's home, I don't think there were any right answers.

January 21: Dear Millicent, how I'd love to run away! Far away. Mother is getting nutzoid. I complained about there not being enough food in the house, and she went postal and yelled and broke my favorite cereal bowl. It was dark blue, the last of a set of four we had back at the old house, the one on

Deodar Street in L.A. I still remember when they were new. I was very young, and I thought they were so beautiful, the bluest blue I'd ever seen. It's a miracle this one didn't get broken a long time ago. I felt really sad about it, for some reason. I know it's not that important, Mill, but we don't have a lot of things left from back then. That was when I used to pretend I had a baby sister.

I cried when that bowl shattered. Cried over a damn bowl! I'm pathetic, Mill.

January 24: Dear Millicent, well, he's done it again. You won't believe it when I tell you. He (my stepfather!) wrecked the Oldsmobile last night. He took it out to "look for work," and then he stopped off at a bar and got stinking, three-sheets-in-the-wind, decks-awash drunk. He hit something—a pole or a tree. He left the car there and got home somehow. Mother was waiting for him. I heard her yelling. He must have been hurt or not feeling too well, because he didn't have much to say.

I don't know how Mother is going to get to work now. He didn't seem very sure just where he'd left the car. As soon as *he* could get up and walk, they went out to look for it. As they left, he was telling her that he'd swerved to avoid hitting a dog. I wonder if that's a better story than the one he told last night.

We're all out of cereal. Looks like I won't be needing a cereal bowl for a while, after all. I had a glass of root beer for breakfast, then called David and bummed a ride to school. I think I'll ask if they can take me with them for a while. David's grandmother is already bringing us back in the afternoon. Mother won't mind; it'll save her time in the morning.

After a long time, my dad got a little more like his old self again. Still, he almost never had time to talk like we used to. Instead, we'd argue a lot about my chores and how much I should help out. One Saturday morning, though, he took me up to Rogers Lake, and we walked around for a while. I wished he'd invited Sharon along, but he was trying to do the dad thing and make some time just for me, without Jason squirming around. It was nice, and the two of us had fun for a change.

Dad and I got to talking about boats. The lake isn't very big, but during the summer, lots of people row or putt around or sail on it. Dad told me that some people buy a boat in the summer and then get tired of it. In winter, they'll take anything for it, just to get out from under the storage or dock fees.

I asked Dad if we could get a little boat. I wanted it for Sharon, really, but I didn't tell him that. He'd think I was nuts over her, or something. He said we didn't have enough room, or enough time, or enough money. Then he told me that he was going to have to work weekends for a while. So no boat. Dad is pretty practical.

But now I knew the best time to buy a boat, if I ever get one.

I told Sharon about my trip to the lake, and about how we could buy a boat cheap in the wintertime. She's very smart. She thought for a while and said "We don't have to have an actual boat. An imaginary one would do . . . at least to start."

"Aren't we sort of old to be playing with make-believe boats?"

"You play computer games, right?

"Uh, right."

"Well, those monsters and robots, are they real?"

"No."

"So why not an imaginary boat, like making up a story."

"I think something real would be better. A rowboat, even."

"Where would we put it? We can't keep it at my place. My stepfather would take it and sell it as soon as we turn our backs. Let's keep our eyes open, and maybe we'll find something."

I didn't like the make-believe boat idea very much. We didn't have time to talk for a few days. I'll let Sharon tell you about what happened next.

CHAPTER 12
OUR BOAT

February 8: Dear Millicent, it turned out the car wasn't too bad. One wheel is all bent, and the fender and headlight are trashed. The front bumper is squashed in on that side, but my stepfather says he has a friend who can fix it. Yeah, sure.

Mother is getting a ride to work with her friend, Angie. I've started riding to and from school with David every day. It's a lot easier this way. Well, okay, Mill, easier has nothing to do with it. I like being with David for a few minutes before and after school.

Mother took me downtown on the bus today to look for stuff at the thrift shops. Cereal bowls, for one thing, Mill. She got three really stupid-looking plastic ones, but they were cheap. And they won't break. Woo-hoo! That's important at our house.

We looked for shoes, but didn't find anything that fit. What I did find was a model sailing ship. It's beautiful! It was only two dollars because there were some pieces missing. Mother got it for me with just a little wheedling. (I think she was still feeling guilty about breaking my favorite bowl.) The boat isn't very big, only 13 inches long, but it's made of several different kinds of wood, some dark, some light. It will do very nicely for our *Silver Dream* until we can buy or find or make something better.

I can't wait to show it to David.

So it wasn't a real boat, but the model had probably cost a lot of money, once. The sails (which were mostly missing) went up and down, like on a real boat, and the rudder and steering wheel worked. I was sold on the idea now. Sharon and I cleared off a space on the workbench in our garden shed and put the *Silver Dream* there, right beside the window, under the 1981 John Deere calendar. Sharon wanted a place to call "the hold." (She was really into boat talk. In case you're wondering, she called the steering wheel "the helm.") I took all the hammers and saws and stuff out of the bottom drawer under the workbench and jammed them into a tool box. *Vwallah*—the hold!

Sharon saw there was a hasp on our drawer. She insisted that we get a lock and fix it so nobody but us could get into "the hold." I found a combination lock that my mom used at the gym after Jason was born. The combination was written on the back. Sharon and I memorized it and then wiped it off. She made a big ceremony of putting the *Silver Dream* in the drawer and locking it. We even shook hands.

Sharon put all that in her diary, along with a few things that were happening at her house.

February 10: Dear Millicent, we launched the *Silver Dream* yesterday. David has a place in his shed where it will be safe. I think we need a log book so we can record our trips and things. Any old book will do—I'll look in the wastebaskets at school. Some good things get dropped in there sometimes.

February 11: My stepfather finally got a job of some kind at a warehouse. He has to take stuff off the shelves. He came home late, real tired, and sat in the kitchen, drinking beer. I tried to tell him I got an A on my geography test, but he kept saying, "Geology. Thass importan' stuff, geology."

Well, maybe we'll have a little money for a change.
Mother bought a cheap can of "shoe stretching spray" at the Factory Super Goof Store. It's supposed to make your shoes fit when they're too tight. I'm not impressed. I guess it helped a little.

Sometimes Jason would forget that Mom was gone. That was awful. We'd be talking about something, and he'd get all worked up and say "Let's show Mom!" or "I'll ask Mom." Once or twice, he even started to look for her. Then he'd remember and start to cry. I'd hug him until he stopped. I felt like crying too, but Jason needed me to be strong, so I didn't.

After our trip to the lake, my dad got real busy at work again, and I didn't have much chance to talk to him, except a little on weekends. He was usually tired from work and grumpy because he hadn't had enough sleep. I knew he missed Mom, too. Sometimes he'd fall asleep reading reports on the couch in the living room. I'd just cover him up with a blanket and let him sleep. I didn't want to bother him. I figured he had enough on his mind, with all the bills and taxes and work and all.

Sharon told me she wanted to sail the *Silver Dream* around the world and have adventures and meet weird people and explore strange places. I mostly wanted to look for treasure. She said that was okay, too.

But then I said I wanted to be captain. That turned out to be not okay. Sharon said she wanted to be "the skipper," that it was her boat, and, besides, she knew more about boats than I did. She was right, but that didn't stop me from wanting to be captain. We argued for about ten minutes, and then Sharon got mad and went home. That upset me, and I wished I'd just given in, instead of being all stupid about it.

Later, she called and said I could be captain when we sail to some countries. She divided up the world and I could have Afghanistan, Austria, Bolivia, Czechoslovakia, Paraguay, Ethiopia, Hungary, San Marino, Uganda, and a lot more places. That seemed pretty fair, so I agreed that she could be captain on trips to all the others. I was so glad she called that I'd have agreed to just about anything.

Sharon felt that, besides the drawer under the workbench ("the hold"), we needed a really secret hiding place. We pulled the drawer all the way out and swept the space between the bottom of the drawer and the floor of the shed. This was our "secret compartment."

At school, Sharon found an old composition book that was only partly used. We cut out the four pages that had been written on, and put "THE LOG OF THE SILVER DREAM" on the front cover with Dymo tape. It looked very official. It went into the secret compartment beneath the bottom drawer in the shed.

About this time, my dad was still working a lot of overtime, like I said earlier, and he started bringing work home again. He'd get home after Grandma and Jason and I had already had dinner. Then he'd go into the den and work on the drawings and papers he'd brought home. I'd go upstairs and help Jason get ready for bed, and then I'd play some computer games with the sound turned all the way off, so it wouldn't wake him up. Even tiny noises would do it. If I remembered, I'd stop playing and try to do my homework. Sometimes I got it all done. Usually I didn't.

For a long time after Mom died, I had this feeling that she was still around. I don't mean like a ghost, hovering around the house. I couldn't quite get it into my head that she was gone. It felt like she was just away somewhere, like maybe Montana or someplace like that. But, of course, I knew she wasn't.

Sharon spent a lot of time at our house to get away from her life at home. I was grateful for that.

February 13: Dear Millicent, things have been quiet lately. My stepfather is too tired from work to do much. He just comes home, drinks, and falls asleep on the couch. Mother doesn't even bother getting him to bed. He snores, and his breath smells like paint or chemicals. *Ewww!*

The car had to have some other things done to fix it. It's worse than it looked, and my stepfather's "friend" didn't do a very good job of fixing it, other than replacing the bent wheel. Big surprise. The right side door doesn't open and close like it used to. When you open it, it goes *"bonk!"* When you close it, it goes *"bwink!"* Half the time, you have to slam it twice to get it to close all the way. The engine is hard to start, and the radiator leaks, too.

We haven't been to the library since forever. Mother hasn't had time. She's trying to save money so she can get another car for him to drive. She's still working two part-time jobs, and has to drop him off at work. She's away a lot. She said I can hang out with David after school until she gets off work, so I don't have to be alone with my stepfather when he comes home.

I cut some new sails for the *Silver Dream* from an old shirt and attached them to the masts. David and I are going to sail around the world, on paper. We'll enter all the ports we stop at in our log book. David will look for treasure wherever we go.

I got a little peeved at him when he wanted to be skipper of the *Silver Dream*. I found the *Silver Dream* and it was mostly my idea. I pretended to be mad and went home and got out my cheap atlas. I made a list of all the land-locked countries in the world and then called David up and said he could be captain when we go to those places. David will catch on sooner or later, but it'll be too late then, Mill! *Muhahaha!*

(I figured it out as soon as Sharon hung up the phone that night. She'd had this sneaky little smiley tone in her voice, so I checked my dad's atlas, and, sure enough, just like Walla-Walla, you can't get to any of those places on a boat. It didn't really matter; we both got to be called "Captain."—David)

CHAPTER 13
VALENTINES AND OTHER TREASURES

February 14: Valentine's day, Mill. I got up early and drew a Valentine's Day card for David. I hope he likes it. I wonder if he'll remember what day it is. Boys don't pay much attention to things like that, Mill. I sort of hope he'll get me a card, though.

I gave Sharon a dumb little paper valentine with a teddy bear on it. She gave me one she drew herself. It had a picture of the *Silver Dream* on the front, and it said "Sail away with me, Valentine," on the inside. Awesome. I still have that card. I'm never going to lose it.

I forgot to bring in the mail when I got home from school that day. Dad brought it in later and tossed it in the basket on his desk. I saw something from school on top of the stack. I thought, *oh no, not another report card!* As soon as he went to the kitchen, I got my jackknife and carefully slit open the end of the envelope. I held my breath and pulled the card out of the brown sleeve inside to take a peek. Disasterville! Worse than last time. Two B's, three C's and a D. Ouch! I just about flipped. I didn't want Dad to get upset. I thought if I could just put it off for another few weeks, I could study my butt off and get my grades back up, and this card wouldn't matter. I promised myself I'd really work harder this time.

But I had to get this sleeve *signed*. I didn't think I could get away with signing it myself, like I'd done last time. Dad had brought this in with the mail, and he must have seen the envelope from school right on top. I had to do something else before he finished getting dinner ready. I had maybe five minutes, max. But what could I do?

Then I had a great idea. Dad keeps my old report cards in one of his desk drawers. I opened the drawer and took out a card from the year before, one with all A's and B's, and put it in the brown sleeve. Then I put everything back in the envelope and glued the end shut before I set it back in the basket. I hoped Dad would just look at the grades and stick the card in his desk with the others. If he checked the date, though, I'd be in deep doo-doo. I hid the new report card in my room.

The next day, I sat with Sharon on the workbench (which was now the "deck" of the *Silver Dream*) and talked about treasures I wanted to search for. It was pretty dumb, mostly. "I'd like to find jewels and pieces of eight, doubloons, gold bars, stuff like that," I told her.

"Okay. Find me a triploon."

"Wait a minute!" I ran up to my room and got a little bag of Hanukkah candy that Alan Wydman had given me, the kind that looks like gold coins. "Here," I told her. "These are triploons."

We put them in the "hold." In the log, we wrote that we'd landed on an island in the Pacific and found pirate treasure. We didn't know any real treasure islands, so we called it *Lottaloot Island*.

A couple of days later, we found that a mouse had gnawed holes in the candy and eaten it. The drawer was yucky. We had to hose it out. So much for my triploons. Sharon said, "Don't worry. It's only money," and we laughed, because it wasn't.

A while after that, the "hold" got stuck. The next time Grandma came over, I asked her to help me get it open. She took a look at it and said the drawer must have got swollen from "someone" getting it wet. We both knew who that someone was. We got it loose and left it out in the sun until it shrank enough to put back, so Dad didn't find out.

The next time we met, Sharon had a little statue of a woman. It didn't have any arms, and not a whole lot of clothes, just like in museums. She told me that it was a valuable work of art, like the *Venus de Milo*. It was sort of pretty. We made an entry in the log of our make-believe trip to Italy, where they have lots of statues like that. We put it in an old cigar box from the garage and called the box our "treasure chest."

Sharon sort of warmed up to the idea of a treasure hunt, silly as the idea was.

February 19: Dear Millicent, David's idea of looking for treasure is fun. So far, we've been to Lottaloot Island and Venice, Italy. We found some very rare gold triploons and a priceless antiquity, the *Venus de Rogersville*. The triploons didn't last long—a mouse ate them. But maybe money isn't the best treasure, anyway. It's not very interesting, and it's so common, Mill. I found the *Venus de Rogersville* in the vacant lot beside the thrift store. I think somebody threw it out, but it's just right for one of our treasures. It has a sort of history behind it.

I took my picture of the *Silver Dream* over to David's and taped it up in his garden shed, over the workbench.

Mother took me to the library again. Ms. Nakagawa, the librarian, let me check out a huge stack of books this time. That felt wonderful, walking out of there with my arms full of books. I checked out three more Elfin-Trek books and four on boats and sailing, and two mysteries, and a book about King Arthur and the knights of the Round Table.

I still missed Mom a lot. It was strange—I'd be going somewhere and I'd think I saw her in the crowd or walking along or in a car. I'd be all excited and happy for half a second, and then I'd see it wasn't really her, just somebody who looked like her a little. I never told anybody about this. They'd have thought I was seeing things or something. But it wasn't like that.

Sharon and I didn't talk much at school. After, we'd sit on the workbench in the shed, beside the little model of the *Silver Dream*, and talk.

"We should look for the greatest treasure of all," she said one day.

"Which one is that?"

"The one that people have looked for for two thousand years—the Holy Grail."

"Is that real? Or is it something somebody made up?"

"There are all kinds of stories about it, so I think it might have been real." She got out a book she was reading and opened it. "Look, here's the story of how King Arthur sent out his knights to search for it."

We looked at the book for a while, and I said, "Okay, I'll add it to my list of treasures to hunt for."

"Some books say the Holy Grail has never been found, but those that searched for it were made better by their quest. Quests are like that. We might not find everything we look for, either, but looking might be important, anyway."

"We should have a bottle with a genie in it, too. Or a magic lamp, like Aladdin. I'll put them on the list."

Sharon found another "treasure." Here's her log book entry for the next day.

LOG OF THE SILVER DREAM, FEBRUARY 23: TODAY WE DROPPED ANCHOR AT THE CITY OF ALEXANDRIA. OUR EXPLORATIONS OF THE RUINS OF THE FAMOUS LIBRARY HERE HAVE REVEALED AN ANCIENT TOME WHICH WE BELIEVE IS THE FAMOUS, LOST "BOOK OF ANSWERS" CONTAINING THE WISDOM OF THE UNIVERSE. WE CAN CONSULT THIS TOME WHENEVER WE DON'T KNOW WHAT TO DO.

NEXT WE WILL SEARCH IN THE NEAR EAST AND THE MEDITERRANEAN FOR ALADDIN'S LAMP. AFTER THAT, THE HOLY GRAIL.

Sharon had brought an old book to the *Silver Dream* that day. It had a splotchy blue and brown leather cover with gold letters on the spine. The leather was real flaky. The pages were brittle, too, all yellow. It was full of words in a foreign language.

"Is it a Bible?" I asked.

"No, it's in Spanish, I think."

"So it could be a *Spanish* Bible."

"It's got an author's name on it, *Quevedo*. I don't think he wrote the Bible."

"What's it about?" I asked.

"I'm not sure. I don't know any Spanish."

"Jose Munoz is a friend of mine. He could translate some of it for us."

Sharon shook her head. "I think it would be better not to know. What if it turns out to be a book about turnips or parsnips or something like that? It's more fun not knowing what it's about. Let's leave it a mystery book."

"Or a book that has the answers to all our questions."

"Yes, that's what it is! *The Magic Book of Answers*."

"Where did you find it?"

"At a garage sale for ten cents."

LOG OF THE SILVER DREAM, FEBRUARY 25: ANOTHER WONDERFUL DAY ABOARD THE SILVER DREAM! CAPT. DAVID AND CAPT. SHARON SAILED AWAY TO CALCUTTA. WE EXPLORED A GROUP OF RUINED PAGODAS OUT IN THE JUNGLE. WE SAW A TIGER AND A DEADLY COBRA, BUT WE DID NOT GET BITTEN, NOR EATEN. OUR NATIVE GUIDE, CHAUNCEY, TOOK US BACK INTO TOWN, WHERE WE SHOPPED FOR ARTIFACTS AT THE MARKETPLACE.

ONE OF THE LOCAL CURIO VENDORS, HABIB, HAD A PAIR OF MYSTERIOUS GLASSES CALLED THE "SPECTACLES OF THINGS-AS-THEY-OUGHT-TO-BE." THE LENSES WERE CUT FROM RARE JEWELS. THE FRAMES ARE MADE OF IVORY WITH LAPIS LAZULI INLAY. THE SPECTACLES MAKE EVERYTHING IN THE WORLD SEEM AS IT SHOULD BE. WHEN YOU LOOK AT UNHAPPY PEOPLE THROUGH THEM, THEY ARE SMILING. WHEN YOU LOOK AT A RUN-DOWN HOVEL LIKE MY HOUSE, IT'S NICE AND CLEAN, AND MERELY "RUSTIC."

HABIB WANTED THREE THOUSAND RUPEES FOR THE SPECTACLES. BUT CAPT. DAVID AND I HAGGLED WITH HIM FOR A LONG TIME AND GOT THE PRICE DOWN TO THREE HUNDRED. HABIB PUT THEM INTO A NEW CASE, JUST LIKE THE ONES FROM THE OPTICIAN'S OFFICE. THE CASE HAD HABIB'S NAME ON IT IN GOLD LEAF: "HABIB'S NEW & USED ANTIQUITIES, CALCUTTA, INDIA."

February 25: Dear Millicent, another treasure day. David found an old pair of sunglasses on the playground near home. The frames were white and the lenses were sort of dark brown. They make things seem warmer when you look through them. We decided they were *The Spectacles of Things as They Ought to Be.* We made an entry in the Log of the Silver Dream and then walked over to the park and took turns putting on the Spectacles and looking at things. They weren't a total success. The lenses are scratched in spots. David was wearing them and running around barefoot, and he stepped in something yucky that squished between his toes. Ick!

After that, we decided that maybe it's better to see things as they are, not as they ought to be. It's okay to see how the world could be, but not to run around in it as if it was already that way. We popped the scratchy lenses out and renamed the frame, *The Spectacles of Things as They Really Are.*

My house looks like the hovel it really is now.

CHAPTER 14
DREAMS, AGAIN

A fter dinner, Dad sat down at his desk to pay bills. He opened the envelope from school, took a quick look at the report card, then put it away in his desk and signed the brown sleeve. He gave me the sleeve to turn in to Mrs. Whitworth and never even noticed that the report card was from a year ago. I was relieved. And sort of not.

Sometimes I'd dream about Mom. The dream was almost the same every time. In it, she didn't die. She sort of got well, but is very weak. She never talks. Everybody is glad she's okay, but we're still very afraid she might die. I feel strange when I wake up, sad that it was just a dream, but better, in a way.

About then, I found an old box full of junk on a shelf in our garage. The last owner must have left it. Inside was a bunch of old nuts and bolts, spark plugs, and a big bronze English coin with a man's head on it and Latin words around the edge.

I showed the coin to Sharon. After our triploon disaster, we decided that this coin was not money. "It's a medal of some sort," Sharon said.

"For doing something brave?" I asked.

"Maybe. I'm not sure. Let's decide later what it's for."

We put the Medal With No Name and the Spectacles and their loose lenses into our treasure chest, and then Sharon went home for dinner. She didn't walk home very fast; I think she didn't want to go.

March 1: Dear Millicent, I went over to David's and we sailed the *Silver Dream* to Alexandria and England for treasure. I wish we could sail away and not come back. Ever.

My mother hit me today for no reason. Not a good reason, anyway. She was waiting for my stepfather to come home after work, and I said something about him coming home drunk again. She got mad and went on about how wonderful he is and all. I said what I thought of him, and then she sort of swatted me. Not very hard, but it hurt. It still hurts, *in here*, Mill.

I finished the first two Elfin-Trek books. They seemed shorter than the others. Or maybe I'm reading faster. Crud.

School was okay. I just went through the motions. Recess was good; I'd talk with my friends about computer games or TV and stuff. Jerry Morris and I swapped more computer games. I got *Sonic Death: Attack of the Saxophones, Mines of Treblon,* and *City Stomper VII: IguanoMan in Akron* from Jerry. He told me some of the cheat codes, too, so I got up the learning curves faster. Yee-hah!

I didn't tell my buddies about the *Silver Dream;* that was secret between me and Sharon. I'd sit near her in class, but we didn't have much chance to talk at school. Every once in a while, we'd look at each other and smile or shrug or make a face. It made the day special.

LOG OF THE SILVER DREAM, MARCH 8: TODAY WE SAILED TO BAHIA, BRAZIL. WE MET ANOTHER TEAM OF ADVENTURERS THERE, BARBARA ("BABOO") AND SCUTTLES MORGAN. SCUTTLES IS A RETIRED PIRATE. HE GETS A PENSION OF 20 PIECES OF EIGHT A MONTH FROM THE PIRATE GUILD, WHICH ISN'T MUCH. HE WORKS PART TIME AS A GUIDE FOR WANDERING COLLEGE PROFESSORS WHO ARE LOOKING FOR ARTIFACTS ON THEIR SUMMER VACATIONS. HE SAYS THEY ARE SMART BUT AREN'T VERY SENSIBLE AND WOULD PROBABLY GET LOST OUT IN THE JUNGLE IF IT WEREN'T FOR HIM.

SCUTTLES SHOWED US ON A MAP WHERE THE SAILING SHIP "GONDWANA GAL" WENT DOWN OFF THE COAST OF BRAZIL IN A HURRICANE

IN 1879. HE SAID HE ALWAYS WANTED TO RAISE HER AND SEE IF THERE WAS ANY TREASURE ABOARD. LEGEND HAS IT (THE DAILY LEGEND, CIRCULATION 12,000, MOSTLY READ BY PIRATES, ADVENTURERS AND COLLEGE PROFESSORS) THAT THERE IS A FORTUNE IN GOLD AND JEWELS IN THE CAPTAIN'S SAFE ABOARD THE GONDWANA GAL.

CAPT. DAVID AND I BOUGHT DIVING GEAR IN RIO AND WE SAILED THE SILVER DREAM OUT TO THE SITE OF THE WRECK. WE WENT OVER THE SIDE IN OUR DEEP SEA SUITS AND SOON LOCATED THE HULL. IT WAS ON ITS SIDE IN DEEP WATER, 200 FATHOMS DOWN. THE MASTS WERE BROKEN OFF AND THE DECKS COVERED WITH SEA URCHINS, CORAL AND BARNACLES. THE RAILS WERE ALL WIGGLING AND FUZZY WITH SEA ANEMONES, AND BARRACUDAS HAD TAKEN UP RESIDENCE IN THE HULL.

CAPT. SHARON LOOKED AROUND ON DECK WHILE CAPT. DAVID WENT INTO THE FORECASTLE AND EXPLORED. HE LOCATED THE CAPTAIN'S CABIN AFT AND SEARCHED FOR THE SAFE. UNFORTUNATELY, THE SAFE WAS NOT FULL OF JEWELS AND GOLD. IT WAS FULL OF I.O.U.'S FROM VARIOUS SEA CAPTAINS AND SAILORS.

AFTER THEY RETURNED TO THEIR BOAT, CAPT. SHARON SHOWED CAPT. DAVID THE BINNACLE SHE HAD RECOVERED FROM THE WRECK. THE COMPASS INSIDE WAS GOOD BRONZE AND CLEANED UP NICELY. IT WAS PROBABLY THE ONLY THING OF VALUE LEFT ABOARD. A BRASS PLATE ON THE SIDE READ,

"MODEL M-2504 MAGIC COMPASS, SER. NO. 3.
DYSON NAUTICAL INSTRUMENT COMPANY,
WALTHAM, MASS. 1875."

VERY FEW OF THESE SPECIAL COMPASSES WERE MADE. THEY DIDN'T POINT NORTH, THEY POINTED IN THE LUCKIEST DIRECTION TO SAIL.

Sharon had bought a compass at a camping supplies store and covered it with plastic "jewels." She said it was magic and could tell you which way to go when you were in doubt. We called it just "The Dyson." When we'd go to the park, we'd always grab The Dyson from the treasure chest and take it along. It actually was sort of useful. If

Jason came along, we'd let him be "The Dyson Carrier." That kept him too busy watching the needle to get into trouble.

That was about when Mrs. Whitworth started in on me about not getting all my homework done. She wrote a letter to Dad and told him I "wasn't applying" myself.

Dad, needless to say, wasn't pleased when he got the letter from Mrs. Whitworth. He got on my case about watching TV, which was no big deal; I wasn't really watching that much. I got kind of angry, and said some things I shouldn't have.

I had no real reason to get mad. I knew he was right about the TV, and I knew he hadn't figured out about the computer games yet.

One night afterwards, I had a funny dream. I was standing in front of a wall in my parents' bedroom. The hospital bed was still there, but Mom was gone. I had a paintbrush in one hand and I was "applying myself." I was dipping the brush into my chest like it was a bucket of paint, and then coating the wall with pink paint. But suddenly there was no more paint in me, and the brush got all dry and stuck to the wall. I felt real bad for some reason and started to cry about it in the dream, but when I woke up it was just another dumb dream, not sad at all, and I didn't know why I was still crying.

I knew I should do the homework, but it always seemed like there was plenty of time to do it before I started and not enough time after. I didn't watch TV much, but when I did, I'd watch any old thing, waiting for the next good show to come on. Dad didn't like it when I did that, but he was usually busy in the den, and I was careful to go upstairs and pretend to do homework before he finished his work.

Things went along more or less the same for a while. I'd get my books and go up to my room; he'd go to the den and work. After I put Jason to bed, I'd play computer games until it got very late or until I heard Dad coming. Then I'd switch to the word processor and do a little homework. I did get some things done. I just didn't get enough done.

CHAPTER 15
THE GLOWING SCREEN CALLS ME

I spent hours and hours on my computer doing role-playing games. Maybe you know how they work—I'd make up a character and take him into this big city where I had to find something. Sometimes I had to find this really big, evil guy. Sometimes he found me. Either way, I had to defeat him or he'd kill my character.

It's a lot of fun, and there's all kinds of good stuff to discover, like gold or armor or weapons and things. Anyway, it's totally interesting, and the scenery and the graphics are just awesome. Whenever my character got "killed," I'd hit a couple of keys, and, *bip*, he was alive again, ready to go on from wherever I'd saved last. It was easy to restart the game.

In fact, it was hard not to. That's what I'm trying to say. The itch to keep going was strong, and I'd restart before I could really think about it. I'd lose track of time and forget everything hurtful in the real world. There was no pain in these games. Maybe I felt a little foolish whenever I got zapped, but I could squash that feeling by starting again right away.

The real world caught up with me finally. The time I wasted on the games sent my grades right down the tube.

Another thing happened right around this time. I was up late, doing some important homework, a report the teacher had told me to turn in *or else*. It was after 10 p.m., and Jason was fast asleep. I was getting real sleepy, myself, when I heard an awful racket coming from Sharon's house. Her parents were having a big ruckus about something. I could hear her mom and dad yelling, and somebody was throwing things. I was afraid Jason would wake up, so I carefully closed the window all the way.

The light was off in Sharon's room, the one at the nearest corner of her house. I wondered if she was asleep. Probably not. I knew she must be hearing it all. It was really loud. That was the first clue I had that all was not okay in Sharon's world. I felt awful about it. And I was curious what they were fighting about. The fight was like TV, only with all the words they leave out on TV.

My dad heard the noise, too, and came into my room. I guess he'd seen that I was still up. I told him I just had to do a little more work and then I'd go to bed. He stood at the window and listened for a while. He told me, "If you can't sleep, you can go into the den and bed down on the couch." But the noise stopped before I was done, so I just flopped into bed.

I didn't know what to say to Sharon the next day about what I'd heard, so I just didn't bring it up. She didn't look too good, and I knew for sure she'd been awake. Nobody could have slept through that yelling. It was like World War III going on.

Sharon had been totally embarrassed. I found this in her diary later:

March 11: Dear Millicent, I'm sure the whole neighborhood heard them fighting. And worst of all, David must have heard them, too! I'm so embarrassed, I could shrivel up and die.

And after all that, my stepfather's been drinking today, again. He started talking to me after dinner. I hate it when he talks to me when he's drunk. If he's not mean and obnoxious, he's all gushy. I get really antsy being around him. He was trying to be nice tonight, but I know if I say the wrong thing, he'll get mad in an instant and swat me or call me awful things.

After he's been drinking, he and my mother stay up late, arguing. A lot of times, she's in a bad mood the next day, and I don't want her to notice me then. I wish I was invisible at school and at home. I need a magic *Cloak of Invisibility!*

March 15: Dear Mill, I heard them fighting again last night. Something about the car. It still doesn't work right. Mother wants him to start putting money aside to replace it. He wants to buy a bigger TV. I sort of like the idea, but I wouldn't want to watch it when *he* is around. I just wish they wouldn't fight. It makes it hard to sleep, and I get sick to my stomach.

I got up and read another book last night. *Unicorn Tracks.* I guess I fell asleep about two o'clock. Now I'm *so* tired. What's going to become of me, Mill?

CHAPTER 16
THE GREAT CLOCK OF NOW

Sharon and I would look for "treasure" whenever we went out, always checking for something that we could pretend was valuable, even if it wasn't. Every day before I went home, I'd check out the waste baskets in the classrooms, just to see if anybody had thrown away anything good. That was where Sharon had found our "log book." I found some perfectly good pencils, once, and another time I pulled a new book out of a waste basket. I never found anything that could be called treasure, though.

Then I thought about Mr. Gardner. He's the custodian at our school, and he also helps keep an eye on things to make sure we're okay. He has a big closet in the basement where he puts stuff that needs to be fixed. After school, I went over to where he was emptying the trash cans.

"Mr. Gardner?"

He looked up at me, but kept working. "Hmm?"

"Do you ever throw out anything good that's almost worth fixing, but not quite."

"Nope. If it's almost worth fixing, I save it for parts. You never know when you might need 'em."

"Oh."

"Anything you need in particular?"

I shrugged. "Just something to play with."

"I see. Well, we can take a look in my good trash bin in a minute." He finished up what he was doing and we went to his closet. He pulled a carton down off a shelf and thrashed around in it. "Here's something," he said. He held up a big, round battery clock that had fallen off the nail and was a little cracked. "This could probably be glued, but I don't have time to do it. Maybe it works, maybe it doesn't. Want it?"

Of course I did. I showed the clock to Sharon later that afternoon in the shed. She liked it. We tried a new battery in it, but the hands stayed stuck on 11:45.

"It doesn't have to actually work to be treasure," Sharon said. "It could be a magic clock that makes time stand still, so you can run around and do things while it stays at whatever time it is for everybody else."

"Yeah, you could stop time during a test so you could go look up all the answers."

"Or if you were late to school, you could stop time until you got there."

"That would be handy. Or maybe you could set the magic clock to any time you wanted and be there, like a time machine."

Sharon asked weird questions. "What is time, anyway?" she said.

I shrugged. "I don't know. It's just there. What I can't figure out is why people say 'a quarter to twelve,' instead of 'eleven forty-five'."

"What's wrong with that?"

"It just always seemed weird to say what time it is by what time it isn't yet."

"People do that a lot, David. We're always thinking about the future."

"Sure. We wonder what's going to happen."

"My mother spends hours wondering what my stepfather is going to do next. Yick. I'd rather think about being grown up and leaving home."

"I worry about my next math test, or how bad I did on the last one. But a lot of times, I think about when Mom was still here. And when she got sick . . . "

"Maybe you should spend more time thinking about *now*, especially when *now* is okay," Sharon said, then added, "or when now is when you're supposed to be doing your homework."

"You, too, Sharon. And we've got the clock to remind us." I held it up and looked at it.

She looked all excited. "That's what it's for, David. That's its magic."

LOG OF THE SILVER DREAM, MARCH 16: YESTERDAY CAPTAIN DAVID FOUND A MAGIC CLOCK WHILE EXPLORING THE DUNGEON OF A CASTLE IN GERMANY ON THE RHINE. IT IS THE FAMOUS GREAT CLOCK OF NOW. IT WAS ASSEMBLED BY AN ECCENTRIC GERMAN CRAFTSMAN, HANS VON GLOCKENSPIEL, IN 1473. WHEN YOU ARE WORRYING ABOUT THE FUTURE OR THE PAST, IT HAS THE POWER TO PUT YOU BACK IN THE PRESENT MOMENT, SO YOU CAN ENJOY HAPPY TIMES. LAST NIGHT, CAPTAIN DAVID fixed THE G.C.o.N. SO THAT EVERY HOUR IS "NOW."

Fixing a new face for the clock had been easy. Dad helped me pop the front off and pull off the hands. Then I turned the old face over and wrote "NOW" twelve times around the dial. When I put it back together again, Dad said it looked great. I sure thought so.

Sharon and I hung the clock over the workbench, beside the old calendar. Whenever we were talking and one of us mentioned unpleasant things that might happen or had already happened, the other one would point at the clock and say, "What time is it, Captain?" Usually that would make us laugh or at least smile.

The schoolwork thing came up right about then. I'd gradually been doing worse and worse in everything. I tried to do my work, but I'd start feeling bad, and the only thing that would take the feeling away was playing computer games. I was in the den, forcing myself to get a science project ready one afternoon, when the phone rang. I picked it up and it was Mrs. Whitworth. I hadn't thought she'd call, which was stupid. It was like I'd thought teachers didn't know how to use phones. I'd figured she'd just keep mailing stuff to Dad, and I'd deal with it when it got here. If I got to the mail first.

Anyway, she says, "I'd like to talk to your father, David."

I was going to tell her he wasn't home, but he came in and said, "Who's on the phone?"

"Uh, Mrs. Whitworth." I handed the phone to him and went on into the kitchen, where we have another extension. I stuck my finger between the receiver and the little button it sits on. Then I lifted up the receiver and slowly took my finger off the gizmo so I could listen in. Mrs. Whitworth was talking:

" . . . didn't want to wait until the progress reports come out, Mr. Greene. I thought I'd give you a call and let you know David is doing very poorly in several subjects. I'd like to meet with you tomorrow after school and talk about it."

"I'm sorry, Mrs. Whitworth, I just can't get away from work. Could we just talk about it now on the phone?"

"If we must. David still isn't applying himself, Mr. Greene. His homework, when he turns any in at all, is very slap-dash, the absolute minimum. His tests are a little better than that, but not enough to give him a satisfactory grade."

"I had no idea."

"If you could just get him to work harder and study more and do all his homework . . . "

"I'll take care of it, Mrs. Whitworth. I'll talk with David tonight."

"Good. I just didn't want you to be surprised when you see his progress report . . . "

I pushed my finger back down on the little button and replaced the receiver. I was in trouble. I ran up to my room as quietly as I could, so he wouldn't know I'd been listening.

Dad came up. He told me what I'd already heard, and said, "David, there'll be no more 'Brain Rotter' until your grades improve. "

"Okay." I didn't mind. I wasn't watching TV that much, anyway, so it was easy for me to go along with what he said. He didn't know it was the computer games that were the problem, not the TV.

"And you'll have to show me your homework every night."

This would have been a very good thing, if he'd remembered to follow up on it. But I showed him two or three assignments, and then he completely forgot about it. I sure didn't remind him. I guess I should have.

Sharon was getting all A's. I don't think she watched TV much. Especially after what happened a few days later.

March 20: Dear Millicent, my illustrious stepfather broke our TV last night. He was watching a basketball game and got mad about something and kicked it. It didn't work very well before, but it doesn't work at all now. I guess he'll say we have to get the big screen TV. Mother put the broken TV out with the trash.

Let's see, Mill: I'm eleven now, I'll be eighteen in seven years and can leave home. I'll become a writer and move to someplace by the ocean like Honolulu or Sydney or San Francisco and write science fiction and fantasy books. I'll have my boat in a marina and, eventually, a big home nearby with woods around it. I won't let my stepfather know where I'm living. I'll send Mother a postcard from time to time.

I need to go to the library again. I've run out of books to read.

March 22: Dear Millicent, Queen Rowena has struck again. I took my shoes off at lunch because they're still too tight. I guess I should have kept an eye on them. When the bell rang, I was in a hurry and I crammed my feet back into them. Ick! Someone (I think I know who) had shoved a half a tuna sandwich in one shoe. First I thought one of the boys had done it—they do stuff like that now. But then I heard Rowena and her toadettes giggle, and I knew they'd been watching me. I hate them all. Especially Betty Lou, that traitor! I'll ignore her for the rest of my life. Or maybe I'll do something nasty to her. And Rowena too, if I can come up with a perfect prank.

When my next progress report came, Dad read it over really carefully. Then he got out my report card file. But, of course, he couldn't find the one from the last time, the one I'd swapped for an old card. I saw him sitting at his desk, going through the papers. "Uh, David?" he said. "Where is your latest report card?"

"I think it's still in the basket with the bills." Then I thought of an even better story and said, "Maybe it got thrown out with the paid bills."

He turned and gave me this look. I could feel his eyes going right inside my head. I should know better than to lie to my dad. He's way too smart. He didn't say anything for a while, just sort of looked at me over his reading glasses. "Oh," he said, "is that what maybe happened?"

I shrugged. "Uh, yeah, maybe."

"Then *maybe* I'd better have Mrs. Whitworth make another copy for us and send it to me at my office." He turned away from me and tossed the papers back into the basket. *Uh-oh*, I thought. I knew right then I was busted.

And speaking of busted, Sharon got in trouble a few days later. It was sort of funny, but sort of not.

CHAPTER 17
SHARON'S ROUGH VOYAGE

March 24: Dear Millicent, today was book report day, and I woke up with a great idea to get back at Rowena Broadburn for the tuna sandwich incident. Yesterday, I saw that her name was on the book report list on the blackboard. At recess today, I waited until everyone went outside, and then I snuck back into the room. I took a piece of chalk and changed the last two letters in her name from "rn" to "tt." Then I pulled the projector screen down far enough to cover the list and ran back outside before Mrs. Whitworth got back from the break room.

It worked, up to a point. When everybody was back in their seats, Mrs. Whitworth said it was time for book reports. Then she saw the screen had been pulled down, so she went over and sent it back up to read the names. Everybody saw "Rowena Broadbutt" and laughed their heads off. Except for Rowena, who just sort of squealed like a pig. That was the high point of my day. Maybe of my whole year.

The low point came right away. Rowena started to cry, because everybody was laughing at her. Mrs. Whitworth wasn't happy about any of this. She went and got an eraser and wiped my handiwork off the blackboard. Then she said, "Whoever did this, please stand up."

As if! I just sat there and wanted to laugh. I bit my lip so I wouldn't. Mrs. Whitworth asked again for the culprit to identify himself. Then she said, "Does anyone know who did this?"

Suddenly everybody was staring at *me*. I wondered why for about five seconds. Then I realized Mary Jane, my trusted friend, had pointed at me and was saying, "I saw Sharon go back into the room during recess." What a Judas!

Well, it was awful, Mill. I lost any cool I ever had. First, I got so nervous, I started to giggle like a lunatic. A *guilty* lunatic. Then Mrs. Whitworth got all frowny and said, "I'm surprised at you, Sharon. You're usually so good . . . " and more along that line. She sent me down the hall to the Principal's office with a note. She even stood at the classroom door and watched me all the way. For some reason, that made me feel really, really wretched, and I started to cry and felt sick to my stomach.

Mr. Furnival (he's the Principal) read the note and looked over his reading glasses at me. Then he gave me a long lecture about respecting others. Then he said I had to apologize to Queen Rowena in front of the whole class. Then I barfed on his carpet.

He called my mother and sent me home. I wanted to crawl into a deep, dark hole.

Mother was not pleased. I thought she was going to slap me, but she just said she was very ashamed of me. I think I'd have rather had the slap.

That was my day, Mill. You still like me, though, right?

Sharon hadn't told me what she was going to do. I'd like to say I'd have talked her out of it if I'd known, but I probably wouldn't have. I thought it was awfully funny. Any funnier, and I'd have wet my pants. We all heard about the puking incident, too. Mr. Gardner had to bring a mop bucket to the Principal's office, and word got around.

Anyway, when Sharon came to school with me the next day, she looked miserable. I didn't talk about what happened. I felt sorry for her later when Mrs. Whitworth made her apologize to Rowena "Broadbutt." Only, of course, she didn't call her that again. I'm afraid some of the other kids did for a while. I guess we were sort of mean.

Things got back to normal in a few days. Sharon and I seemed to sail away a little more often, though.

CHAPTER 18
THE GRAIL

Log of the Silver Dream, March 29: Today Capt. David and I explored an ancient monastery in Jerusalem. Behind a wooden panel, we found a secret door leading to the catacombs below the monastery. Our search took us deep, deep into a series of underground chambers.

After much searching, we discovered a hidden passageway to the tomb of a holy man, St. Nefrusius, who died in 155 AD. The tomb was creepy and dark and smelled awful. Right in the middle, there was a big sarcophagus where they'd put the holy man. On top of it was a smaller chest with iron bands around it and a big keyhole.

We picked up the chest and carried it between us all the way back up to daylight. Once we got lost and were afraid we'd never find our way out, but we did. When we got out, we spent several hours picking the lock. At last the chest opened, and inside, as shiny as the day it was made, was the authentic, genuine Holy Grail, all wrapped in deep purple velvet. It's a small, shallow wine cup made of silver.

King Arthur would have been proud of us and knighted us on the spot, if he'd been there. "Arise, Sir David and Sir Sharon, Knights of the Realm," he'd have said.

SAIL AWAY ON MY SILVER DREAM

WE TOOK THE GRAIL BELOW AND STOWED IT IN THE VAULT, WHERE IT WILL STAY SAFE IN OUR KEEPING FOREVER.

The two of us spent more time treasure hunting. My friends Jerry and George's dads let me go through the junk in their garages. Once, right after school, we went downtown with Mrs. Quandres to make the rounds of the thrift stores on Main Street. While Sharon's mom shopped, Sharon and I wandered along, searching for things to use as treasure.

"Let's go in here," she said. "They have nice things."

"Okay. Maybe too nice. I've only got seventy cents." I looked around and whispered, "Where do you think they keep the grails?"

She laughed. "Ask the clerk, silly."

I was too chicken to ask. "He'll probably want to know whether we want Regular grails or Holy ones."

We got to giggling, and the guy behind the counter frowned at us and pointed at the door, so we had to go laugh outside.

The store next door had awful prices. I guess they hoped a movie company would come in and buy all their crap to make a film about the sixties. We stayed there just long enough for Sharon's mom to catch up with us, and then we moved on down the street.

In the third store, the stuff was really junk, but it was cheap.

"Salvation Army rejects," Sharon said. We wandered around. I was looking for things like big chalices and fancy cups. Sharon headed for a bunch of cardboard boxes in the back, piled full of all sorts of trash. It was pretty grungy, most of it. She found a bunch of dirty old plant crocks stacked in a box. Inside the top crock was a little metal dish about three inches across. It was blackish, dimpled in the middle, with a handle ring on one side and a little kind of saddle on top of that.

"It's an ashtray," I said.

Sharon shook her head. "No, I don't think so. The bottom's all bumpy. It would be too hard to clean if you put ashes in it. And look, there's a little link in this hole in the handle. It looks like it was attached to something else, like a chain."

"Yeah, they chained the ashtray down so nobody could steal it."

"It's *not* an ashtray. It's a grail. We should buy it."

The guy at the front of the store came back and asked if we had any questions.

"What's this for?" I asked him, holding up the metal dish.

"It's a ashtray," he said.

I grinned at Sharon.

"How much is it?" she asked.

"Uh, a dollar."

Sharon looked at him. "Mmm. How about fifty cents?"

I paid, and the man put the little dish into a bag.

As we went to find her mom, Sharon whispered to me: "This is our Grail."

"But it's too small for a grail. It won't hold much wine."

"It's not for guzzling out of, David. It's a *symbol!*"

When we got back to my house, we took the ashtray into the kitchen and washed it with soap and water. It got a little less dull, but was still very dark. Then I tried some silver polish from under the sink, and in two minutes the dish was shiny all over.

"See? It's silver!" Sharon said. "A grail."

"Or a silver ashtray."

Grandma Greene was in the living room with Jason, so we showed her the little dish. "This is an ashtray, isn't it, Grandma?"

She looked it over. "No, David. It's what a wine steward uses to taste a bottle of wine when it's first opened. This link is where it attaches to a chain around his neck. It's the steward's badge of office."

"It's a little wine cup?"

"Yes, but you'd better stick to grape juice."

Sharon really rubbed it in. "Ashtray, huh? *I told you!*"

We took our grail out to the *Silver Dream* and put it in the treasure chest, which Sharon now insisted be called "the vault" from then on. "You don't put a Holy Grail in a *treasure chest*. You put it in a *vault*."

We weren't sure what to do with a Holy Grail. We looked through the King Arthur book that Sharon got from the library, but didn't find anything. Sharon thought it was good for curing sick people or something.

My dad got home this one night, and right away he whipped out a copy of my real report card, the one I'd tried to keep him from seeing. "Mrs. Whitworth mailed this to me at my office," he said. "What about this? This sure doesn't look like the one I saw earlier." He put on his reading glasses.

I shrugged.

He kept going: "This says you got two B's, three C's and a D. The version I saw was all A's and B's. Can you shed any light on this mysterious change?" He looked at me over his reading glasses, waiting.

I tried the most innocent reason: "Uh, the new card must have got mixed up with an old one."

"Oh, really? And where did the new one go?"

I knew he had me cornered. The longer I struggled, the worse he'd make it. I gave in. "Well, I hid it, because it really stank."

"It sure did." He held his copy of the report card out as far as he could reach and waved it. "I can smell it from here. So, what do you propose we do about this? What would you do if you were me?"

I hate it when he says that. I always end up saying the same thing he wants. I tried anyway: "No TV for a month?"

"That might be a good start, except you already lost your TV privileges until your grades go back up. This isn't just about grades, it's also about dishonesty. Swapping the cards may have seemed clever, but it wasn't the honest thing to do. I think we need something more drastic than no TV for a month."

I made another feeble try: "No TV for two months?"

He smiled and shook his head slowly from side to side. "David, I think you need a rest from your computer games. No *World of the Beastulons* for a month. That goes for *Lundgren vs. The Ants* and *Trunnions Over Ploesti*, too. And *Fortress World of Doom*."

"Aw, Dad!" I was hoping an "aw, Dad" would head off more damage. And it did. He'd only named four games, and I'd already played them until they were boring. I had been playing *Beastulons* a lot for a week, but I'd finished it a couple of days before. *Lundgren* wasn't that great, no big deal. *Trunnions Over Ploesti* I'd miss a little, but I had others not on Dad's list that I hadn't finished. And he didn't know about *Megilla Carter Meets Algol Thorblod*, or *Density*, or *Age of Ennui*, which were in my backpack. I'd just gotten them from Jerry Morris that same day, in trade for *Beastulons*.

I knew I still wasn't being really honest, and I paid for it later. But there was no way Dad would ever catch me playing the new games. About halfway up the stairs, there's this step that has a loose board and makes a funny noise when anybody steps on it. If I heard that step creak, I'd toggle back to the word processor and start typing like a fiend. By the time Dad got to the top of the stairs and back down the hall to my room, I looked like I'd been doing homework for hours. I was sure this would keep him from catching me.

That night, I found a picture of Mom in my desk drawer and put it in my wallet. I wasn't sure why.

Meanwhile, Sharon was sad about not having any friends at school. Except for me.

March 31: Dear Millicent, school is the pits. I don't really have anybody to talk to. I refuse to get my eyeballs dirty by even looking at Mary Jane, the Benedict Arnold of my school. I get to talk to David, though, a little more. He knows I don't have any friends, now, so he comes over and says hello at lunch and recess.

Today, he showed me a picture of his mother. I only saw her a few times. He said he wished I'd met her before she got so sick. I think he still misses her a lot, Mill. Some days, he's just like he was right after she died. He seems *adrift*.

Sharon and I talked about sailing almost every day. She knew a lot about it now. One day, we were waiting on the lawn in front of the school for my dad to pick us up. "Is sailing dangerous?" I asked her.

"Not very. I've read three books about it from the library. It's safe if you know what you're doing." She picked a dandelion puff.

"What if you run into something?"

"There's not much to run into on the open sea, maybe a coral reef or something like that. You can usually see waves splashing against them. At night, you can hear them before you hit them. Most of them are charted."

"What about icebergs?"

Sharon blew the puff and sent the seeds flying out over the lawn. "You only have to watch for icebergs in certain latitudes. Most of the time, anyway. But we'd keep watch if we had the sails up. And, besides, you can get warnings over the radio."

"Last year, a teacher told us only about 10 percent of an iceberg shows; the rest is under the water where you can't see it."

Sharon was quiet for a while and then said, "People are like icebergs, too. There's a lot to people we don't see."

"You mean, inside our minds?"

"Yes."

"So, what do you think it's like at the bottom of your mind-berg?"

She smiled. "Like an ice palace, all blue-green and quiet, like the sea, full of mysterious things."

"What kind of things?"

"Oh, things I've forgotten . . . mind-treasures . . . dreams . . . and elf magic!"

CHAPTER 19
THE RING OF TRUTH

Sharon and I were out in the garden shed, just talking about things. "Jose Munoz says his dad used to be a Mountie," I said.

"Mmm. I don't think that's true."

"Why not?"

"I don't know," Sharon said. "It just doesn't have the ring of truth."

"Ring of truth?"

"Yes. People say something has 'the ring of truth,' when it sounds like it's probably true."

"Maybe people say that 'cause there used to be a magic 'Ring of Truth' that made it so you couldn't lie when you were wearing it. "

"That'd be useful," Sharon said. "Judges in olden times could make people put the ring on before they spoke. Maybe we'll find a Ring of Truth the next time we sail somewhere on the *Silver Dream*."

I looked around in the shed and the garage for something ring-ish. I found a short piece of brass tube just the same size as my finger, so I cut a ring off one end with Dad's hacksaw. I scraped the ring on the sidewalk to smooth it off and then rounded the edges with some fine sand paper. Vwallah! The Ring of Truth!

Later, Sharon took a sharp nail and scratched "runes" around the outside of the ring. She'd copied them from one of the Hobbit books. I liked it a lot.

LOG OF THE SILVER DREAM, APRIL 1: CAPT. DAVID AND CAPT. SHARON SAILED THE CARIBBEAN TODAY AND VISITED ONE OF THE PIRATE TOWNS THERE. THE LOCAL AUTHORITIES GAVE US PERMISSION TO TOUR THE FORTRESS WHERE THEY KEEP THEIR TREASURES. THE FORTRESS HAS AN IMMENSE AND VERY OLD UNDERGROUND MAZE BELOW IT, ITS WALLS DECORATED EVERYWHERE WITH RICH CARPETS AND TAPESTRIES AND FLAGS TAKEN FROM CAPTURED SHIPS.

THE MAZE IS SO OLD, NONE OF THE PIRATES KNOW WHEN IT WAS CONSTRUCTED. WE ALMOST FELL INTO A DEEP WELL GOING DOWN, DOWN INTO THE DEPTHS OF THE FORTRESS. WE SHINED OUR FLASHLIGHTS DOWN THE SHAFT. CAPT. DAVID NOTICED THE GLINT OF SOMETHING SHINY FAR BELOW US. WE LOWERED OURSELVES BY OUR ROPES AND DISCOVERED AN ELABORATE GOLDEN RING AT THE BOTTOM OF THE WELL. I RECOGNIZED IT IMMEDIATELY AS THE FAMOUS RING OF TRUTH FASHIONED BY THE FIRST DYNASTY PHARAOH "SHETEP YUSEF." I PUT IT ON AND WE STARTED TO WALK BACK TO OUR SHIP.

I'D HOPED TO SMUGGLE THE RING OUT OF THE FORTRESS WITHOUT BEING DETECTED. UNFORTUNATELY, JUST AS I THOUGHT WE WERE GETTING AWAY, ONE OF THE PIRATE GUARDS MET US AT THE EXIT. "DID YOU FIND ANYTHING INTERESTING?" HE ASKED.

I WAS WEARING THE RING, SO I HAD TO TELL THE TRUTH. I IMMEDIATELY SAID, "YES, WE FOUND SHETEP YUSEF'S ANCIENT AND EXTREMELY VALUABLE RING OF TRUTH, WHICH I'M STEALING EVEN AS WE SPEAK."

"OH, HA HA, YOU ARE SUCH A JOKER," THE GUARD SAID, AND WE LAUGHED AND SAID, "GOODBYE," AND WALKED RIGHT PAST HIM.

THE RING OF TRUTH WILL JOIN THE HOLY GRAIL IN OUR VAULT.

A few days later, we were talking in the shed. Sharon was sitting on the workbench, playing with the Ring of Truth, slipping it on and off her finger. She had small hands, so it was loose.

I was standing in front of her and reading the log book. "Where should we sail next?" I asked.

"Mmm, someplace very exotic, I think. Let's go to Nogottatoga."

"Where's that?"

She thought for a minute, then said, "Nogottatoga is halfway between the Sandwich Islands and the Pizza Archipelago. The natives there are friendly brown people, with big smiles, and they laugh a lot. They live in grass huts and never wear shoes, and they swim in the ocean every day."

"They sound nice."

"Yes. They really care about visitors and they always ask if they're happy." Sharon got very quiet. She didn't look happy. In fact, she looked sadder than I'd ever seen her.

"Sharon?" I put the log book down on the bench.

She lowered her head, and I could see a tear running down her cheek.

"Are you happy?" I asked. It was a stupid question, I guess, and I knew what the answer would be, but I had to ask anyway.

"Y . . . y . . . yes . . . " she started to say. Then she looked down at the Ring of Truth on her finger and said "No! The truth is, I'm absolutely miserable!" She started crying.

For a few seconds, I was sorry I'd asked. What a dumb question! Then I got to feeling the way I did at my mother's funeral—I wanted to just run away.

But I couldn't leave Sharon. "Everything will be all right," I said. Mom used to tell me that sometimes. Now I didn't believe it anymore. Mom died, so things *weren't* all right, and they might not turn out okay for Sharon, either. When I thought about that, my eyes got all blurry and I felt a little sick.

Sharon just kept sobbing. I couldn't think of anything more to say, and I knew if I just stood there, I'd cry, too, so I moved closer and put my hand on her arm. She leaned her head against my shoulder.

It was a long time until she stopped crying. By then, I had both arms around her. When she sat up straight and opened her eyes, I got all embarrassed and stood back while she wiped her eyes. Well, I had to wipe mine, too, to tell the truth.

We didn't say anything for a while.

"My father is a drunk," she said. "He gets drunk every night, and then he and my mother fight."

"I . . . " I almost said, "I know," but thought it might embarrass Sharon even more if she knew I'd heard him yelling and breaking things that night. "I'm sorry," was all I could say.

"He hits my mother, too. He took all the rent money once, and spent it on an old motorcycle. We don't have any money, so I have to dress in used clothes, like a complete dweeb. The girls at school all hate me. A couple of weeks ago, one of them shoved a tuna sandwich into my shoe while I wasn't looking."

"Rowena Broadbutt?"

"Or one of her toadettes. She was watching me when it happened."

I remembered the book report incident. "So that's why you . . . "

"Yes. Payback. It seemed like a really good idea at the time."

I came very close to laughing, but kept a straight face, somehow.

"My so-called friend, Mary Jane, ratted on me. Then I got sent to the Principal's office. I'm getting an Unsatisfactory in Behavior on my next report card, on top of it. Mother is mad at me. None of the other girls talk to me. And Mr. Furnival is still upset about his carpet. No, I'm not happy."

I thought about Mr. Furnival frowning over his carpet, and I laughed. *Oops.* "I'm sorry. I didn't mean to laugh."

Sharon gave me a brief smile. "It's not your fault, David. Thank you for asking. You're a true friend."

A true friend. Those words should have made me happy. In a way, they did, but somewhere inside, I felt sad. I wanted Sharon to stay with us and not go home, ever.

She wiped her nose and sniffed and gave another little half sob. "I must look a real mess."

"Your eyes are all red. Come inside and wash your face."

Sharon went in and washed, and I gave her a glass of soda. Her mom came to get her a minute later, so we didn't get to talk any more.

Afterward, I wished there was something I could do to help Sharon, but I couldn't think of anything. I decided the best thing I could do was to look for a really awesome treasure to give her the next time we sailed together. Then I thought of something.

I'll let Sharon tell you what I came up with:

April 8: Dear Millicent, today David and I were in his living room after school, and he got real quiet. Nervous quiet. I could tell he was excited. Then he reached into his pocket and held out a tiny box and said: "Here. This is for you. It's a special treasure."

I opened the box. Inside, there was a little silver pin shaped like an angel. There was a real ruby in it, too, and a few rhinestones. Nobody ever gave me anything that nice, Mill. Ever.

"It's a guardian angel," he said, "to protect you."

I hugged him. "Thank you, David. It's beautiful."

He turned red and looked down at his feet. I was so happy, I was almost weeping, but I tried not to let him see. He might think I'm just a sappy girl. David is so good. I am lucky he's my best friend, Mill.

I'll have to hide the angel pin so my mother and stepfather don't see it. I must keep it forever. Now I *am* getting weepy, Mill.

April 9: Dear Millicent, Mother took me to the library again, finally! I got fourteen books: four more Elfin-Treks, two more books on sailboats, a book about dragons, a science fiction trilogy, and some picture books of far-away places. I wish I was all grown up and could go and live by myself in somewhere far away, like Nogottatoga.

They had old National Geographics at the library for fifteen cents. One still had a big map of the world folded up in it! I bought it for the Silver Dream.

Mother also got me some new(er) tennies. They are sort of cheap and probably won't last long. (There I go, living ahead of the clock!) I'll try not to wear them out before school ends. At least I can actually lace them up, and they have daisies on them. The waffle-stompers are history. I hope the weather doesn't get cold again.

April 15: Dear Millicent, I had another of those dreams about my doll, Emily, being real. She was *so* real! I could even see her drool, and everything. Why would I dream such a weird thing? In the dream, I hugged Emily and told her I loved her and that I was glad she was alive again. She smiled at me, Mill. It makes me cry to remember her little smile.

Sharon had showed me the world map she'd bought. We'd put it up on the back of the shed door. I got some push pins from Dad's desk, and we stuck them in the map wherever we'd sailed the *Silver Dream*. There were a lot of pins. Afterwards, we sat out on the grass in the backyard and talked.

Sharon told me about these "weird dreams" she had. They didn't sound scary, but they must have bothered her. I told her the dream about where I'm "applying myself" with a paintbrush. It made her laugh, so I didn't tell her the part about crying when I ran out of paint.

She said that when she was little, she used to believe that her doll could move around and burp and stuff, like a real baby. I don't know if I ever could think up things like that. I thought, *Sharon sure has a great imagination. Maybe she's always been that way, and that's how she made up an imaginary sister.*

CHAPTER 20
ANSWERS

I t was raining one day in April. Sharon and I stayed in the shed after school, sitting on the workbench and just looking out the window at the rain on the bushes and trees in our backyard.

"My father hit my mother really bad last night," Sharon said. "She had a black eye this morning."

"That's awful." I wondered what it would have been like if my dad had hit Mom. *Horrible*, I thought. It made me cringe to think about it.

"I'm afraid of him," Sharon said.

"I would be, too."

Sharon nodded. "The morning after he hits her, he always promises he'll never do it again. And she believes him! Later, he gets drunk and goes right ahead and hits her. Then he says it was her fault. What are we going to do?"

I sure didn't know. I wished that I had a clue. My father hardly ever drank, and he never hit my mom. I don't remember him even spanking me, even though I was worse than Jason when I was little. Anyway, I didn't know what Sharon should do, so I said, "How about the *Book of Answers*? Maybe it will tell us the right thing to do."

Sharon agreed with this, stupid as it may seem. I got the *Book of Answers* out of the hold and held it up to my forehead. "Oh, great *Book of Answers*, tell us what Sharon should do." I opened it up at random, and, of course, there was nothing but a page of Spanish words looking at me. Me, who speaks only English. (Except for *bueno* and *amigo*, and a few special words that Juan and Jose taught me.)

The page might as well have been blank. I didn't know what to say, so I pretended to read, mumbling this and that, sounding out a word from the page here and there. I made my mind blank. Suddenly, I knew what to say. "*The Book* says we're looking in the wrong book."

"What?" Sharon said.

"Yeah, the Book says the answer to your question is in *another* book. At the library. You just have to go there and find the right book."

"Hmm. That's not a big help. How am I going to know what's the right book?"

"You could ask the librarian. She's nice. Maybe she'll help you."

Sharon tilted her head and looked at me. "No way I'm going to go up to Ms. Nakagawa and say, 'Hey, my father likes to punch my mother. Have you got any books on how to keep her from getting hit?'"

She was right. I said, "We ought to go and just look, anyway. Maybe we'll get lucky, like we did with the Grail."

I asked Dad if he could take us to the library. He'd been after me to study more, so he couldn't very well say no. Sharon went home and got some books to return, and half an hour later we were at the downtown library. Dad went to look at some techie mags and Sharon and I were on our own.

I pointed at the librarian and whispered, "There's Ms. Nakagawa. Go ask her."

"You ask her. I'm too chicken."

"Uh, let's get some other books, first. Then we'll ask."

We scouted around and, totally by accident, I found a book on what we were studying in Social Studies. Sharon got four more fantasy novels, the kind she likes about elves and dragons. Then we walked up and down the non-fiction aisles, looking for books that might help Sharon. No luck there.

We gave up and went up to check our books out. Then we just stood there at the desk. I nudged Sharon. She nudged me back.

Ms. Nakagawa must have been watching us. "Do you have a question? Do you need help finding something?"

Sharon suddenly wasn't there. She had moved swiftly and silently away from the desk, leaving me standing there, alone. My heart stopped, but I couldn't let Sharon down. This was the just about hardest thing I'd ever had to do.

"Uh, I have a friend whose dad hits her . . . uh, *his* mom a lot. Do you have anything that can help?"

"I think I do," Ms. Nakagawa said. "Wait right here." She went down to the far end of the library and came back with two books. She checked the books out on my card. "Give these to your friend. They're due back in three weeks, but come and see me if there's any problem."

I thanked Ms. Nakagawa. I was nervous, so I didn't do a very good job of it.

I collected all my stuff and Sharon, and said, "Let's go." We went and got my dad to drive us home. When we dropped Sharon off in front of her place, I handed her the two books, and she put them in her backpack. I waved at her when she got to her door.

April 21: Dear Millicent, David and his father took me to the library tonight. I didn't have the nerve to ask the librarian for help and I ran away, but David stayed at the desk and asked her for books to help me. He didn't say they were for me, though.

Ms. Nakagawa gave him two books: one is called *Family Violence* and the other is *Courage To Be Me*. That last one's about parents who drink too much. How did she know about the drinking, Mill?

Log of the Silver Dream, April 22: Today, Capt. Sharon honored Capt. David and awarded him the prestigious "Medal for Not Running Away" with a blue ribbon for being a true-blue friend when it wasn't easy.

My next report card came on a Friday. It wasn't very good. In fact, it was the worst ever. I got a B in P.E., but two C's and three D's in everything else. I took the card into Dad's office in the den and put it on his desk. Well, he hit the roof when he saw it, called Mrs. Whitworth, and went in to see her. She gave him the full story, which was still no homework and lots of lousy test scores.

The only thing that kept me from getting all D's was stuff I'd worked on with Sharon after school. I'd picked up a little Geography from our big map in the shed and the book I'd checked out at the library that time with Sharon. Once in a while, if we knew her mom was going to be late, Sharon and I would take our books out to the *Silver Dream* and do our homework together. Otherwise, I'd try to squeeze it in between computer games and bedtime. If I was desperate, she'd let me copy some of her homework before school. She wasn't real happy about that, so I didn't do it every week.

Anyway, Dad stomped upstairs, turned on my computer, found all my games and deleted them. He took the disks, too, and the manuals. I got really, really mad and tried to stop him. That was dumb. I knew he was right, but I was mad anyway. It was like I was angry that he didn't trust me, even though I wasn't very trustable.

Does that make sense? Heck, no. I guess I was mad at myself, for not being able to stop playing and study. The fact that he was right only made it worse—I felt like throwing things, but I didn't. Mostly I just yelled and whined and jumped up and down. I finally stopped when I realized I was acting like Jason at his worst.

I was afraid the games were gone for good. I asked when I could get them back, and Dad said as soon as my grades were back to normal. That was a relief. But I was still pretty upset. No more zoning out after dinner.

Sharon used to zone out, too, but she did it with books, and I don't think reading ever was bad for her.

April 27: Dear Millicent, I've read the books from the library on abuse and alcohol. Things are going to get worse, Mill, and there's nothing I can do to stop it. I don't know how to get my mother to read the books. I thought I'd just leave them for her to find. But he might see them before she does.

Mill, if we stay here, I'm afraid of what will happen. He started slapping her this morning at breakfast, right there with me watching. I wanted to stop him, but I couldn't move. I was too afraid. I just sat there. He finally knocked her down and kicked at her, but missed and stumbled and almost fell. He stomped out of the house then.

April 28: Dear Millicent, Mother had to go to the emergency room yesterday morning. After she got to her job, she was too hurt to work. My stepfather had the car, so she had her friend Angie take her to the hospital. She sprained her elbow or her shoulder or something yesterday when he knocked her down. The doctor took an x-ray, put a sling on her arm and sent her home. When I got back from school, she told me what happened. I thought this would be a good time to give her the books. I just handed them to her and went to my room.

She came up a few minutes later and threw the books at me. She yelled: "Your father's not an alcoholic! He just has a little drinking problem."

I couldn't believe my ears, Mill. She's *clueless*. What will it take for her to see what he's like? What's going to become of me, Mill?

CHAPTER 21
WHAT WILL IT TAKE?

April 30: Dear Millicent, Mother went to the hospital, again, yesterday. *He* knocked her around in the living room last night after dinner. She couldn't get out of his way because of the sling she's wearing, and I tried to help her because she couldn't defend herself. That was a mistake. He turned and took me and threw me against the wall. He was going to punch me, too, I think, but Mother shouted, "Remember Deodar!" That's the street we used to live on in Los Angeles. He left me alone and told her to shut up. I wanted to punch him, but I started to cry instead. He kicked at her a couple of times and then went out and drove away.

I helped her up. She was more worried about me than about herself. She kept saying "I'm sorry, I'm sorry," like it was her fault that he threw me around. In a way, I guess maybe it was. We shouldn't be here.

She was bleeding where he hit her in the face. We tried to clean her up and get her ready for bed, but she was having trouble breathing, so I called Angie and she drove us to the hospital.

The emergency room was a zoo. There were about a kajillion people wandering around, or sitting, or lying on tables.

And half their relatives were there, too. Babies were screaming. We had to wait over an hour before the doctor took care of Mother. After he'd looked her over, the doctor called a policewoman, but Mother wouldn't talk to her. I thought that was a mistake. The policewoman said she wanted the doctor to check me, too, but I said I was okay. Just then, some man came in who'd been shot, so the doctor never got around to me. A nurse put some dressings on Mother and gave her some pills and we went home.

My stepfather was still gone, thank God. I helped Mother into bed, and she said, "I think you'd better bring me those books again, honey."

Later, she fell asleep reading, and I hid the books under my bed where *he* wouldn't see them if he came home. Then I wedged a piece of wood under my door before going to bed.

As I was putting on my jammies, I found I had bruises on my arm and my side and more on my back, where I hit the wall.

I wonder what she meant by "Remember Deodar."

Sharon told me the next day what had happened. She was pretty upset. I was afraid for her. After school, at home, we got out the Holy Grail, and she held onto it while we talked some more. She cried a little. I put an arm around her carefully, because of her bruises, and held her hand for a while. She and her mom needed help, but I didn't know what to do.

It turned out, I'd already helped a lot. Me and Mrs. Nakagawa.

May 2: Dear Millicent, my mother and I went to an Al-Anon Family Groups meeting last night. Al-Anon is a support group for friends and relatives of alcoholics. She took me along because she didn't want me home alone in case *he* showed up. She cried a bunch, and one of the women talked with her after the meeting for a long time. There were lots of people there, Mill. They were very nice. It reminds me of Nogottatoga.

Everybody seems to care how you *feel*. I felt *hopeful*. Maybe things will be okay.

I hope we'll go back to the Al-Anon meeting again. I also hope my stepfather doesn't find out. Things can't go on this way. It's too dangerous.

Sharon was going through a lot of trouble herself, but she still was worried that I was getting awful grades in school. Sometimes we'd talk about it aboard the *Silver Dream*. For a couple of weeks after the report card disaster, school went okay. It was a struggle, but I got my stuff in on time and got a few okay grades on tests.

Then I found that Dad had missed one old, old game on my computer, *Mind-Sweeper*. I was totally jazzed when I found it. As games go, it's pretty simple, but, hey, it's a game. I slipped right back into the same old thing: *Mind-Sweeper* for endless hours, then panicky minutes of getting a few paragraphs down on paper to turn in the next day for school.

Sharon and I were in the shed after school one day, talking. "I didn't do so hot today," I said.

"Yes, I noticed. You didn't put your hand up to answer any questions at all. I saw Mrs. Whitworth looking right at you a lot."

"I tried to do my homework last night, but when I sat down with my books in front of me, I felt real tired, and it hurt just to think. I got this urge to do something else, anything else."

"So what did you do?"

"Uh, I turned on the computer and opened the word processor."

"So it would look like you were doing homework, right? And then?"

"And then I played *Mind-Sweeper* for an hour."

"How long, David?"

"Well, two hours. Maybe three."

Sharon frowned at me. "David! Why didn't you stop?"

"I zoned out completely. It was like I stopped hurting somewhere inside while I was in the game."

"You've got to study! We need to consult the *Book of Answers* to see what to do to make your grades better." She got the book out of the bottom drawer and held it up to her forehead. After a minute, she said, "What you need is a Thinking Cap that will make it easier to study."

"A cone-shaped one?"

She snorted and pretended to laugh. "Ha-ha. No."

"Okay, what can we use for a Thinking Cap?"

"Mmm. I'm not sure. Give me a day or two. In the meantime, let's move the Great Clock of Now up to your room."

We took the clock upstairs and hung it on the wall over the computer, right where I could see it. The next few nights, I'd look at the clock every time I saved the game, and sometimes I'd even stop playing and shut the computer down. That helped some, but I still played way too much, as my grades showed.

May 10: Dear Millicent, David got a really bad report card last month. He's been doing nothing but play computer games after dinner. I don't know why. He's very smart and he used to get good grades. He just seems to hate doing homework this year. I think it has something to do with losing his mother.

I found a baseball cap in our old clothes bag. I ran it through the washer and put *THINK* on the front with an indelible marker. That will be our Thinking Cap. I'll take it aboard tomorrow and give it to David. I hope it works.

My stepfather said he was too sick to go to work today. The truth is, he was hung over from last night. At least he didn't start hitting us again. Yet.

Sharon gave me the Thinking Cap with a big ceremony, and put an entry in the log about it. After she went home that afternoon, I decided I needed to quit playing *Mind-Sweeper* for sure until summer vacation. I thought maybe if I put on my Thinking Cap and worked on my homework really hard, I'd be able to do without the game.

Log of the Silver Dream, May 11: Today, Capt. Sharon presented Capt. David with a genuine, 500 watt, brain-boosting "Thinking Cap." It raises the wearer's IQ by 50 points, making it easier to do homework and other stuff you'd rather not do.

I was okay for that first night. I thought about the imaginary extra 500 watts in my head and got all my work done early. I went right to bed and slept well. But the next morning, I didn't want to get out of bed. I was in a bad mood, and school was awful. After school, as soon as Sharon went home, I knew what would make me feel better. I ran upstairs and played *Mind-Sweeper* for hours.

Dad came up twice to check on me, but the squeaky step gave him away both times, and I was into the word processor before he stuck his head into my room. I didn't even look at the *Great Clock of Now*. I finally shut down the game about midnight and did a little homework. So much for quitting. I felt ashamed.

Sharon was still having her strange dreams.

May 11: Dear Millicent, another dream. This time I'm pushing a stroller with Emily in it. She's reaching out and trying to pick the flowers along the sidewalk in front of our old house. I'd forgotten all about those flowers. Daisies, hundreds of them. Mother planted them. Funny how I remember that. I don't remember much about when I was small. It's mostly a blank.

We had a few minutes to talk during lunch on a Wednesday. Sharon told me again how she was having the Emily dream. "What do you think it means?" she asked.

"I don't think dreams mean anything. I think they're just something your brain does at night to keep from getting bored."

"You mean, after you go to sleep, your brain turns on the Dream Machine?"

"Yeah. It plays movies," I said.

"But where does it get them?"

I shrugged. "I don't know."

Sharon thought for a little bit, then said, "Maybe they come from deep down in our minds."

"From the bottom-of-the-iceberg part of you?"

"Yes," Sharon said. "In the Ice Palace, there's a movie library. That's where all our memories are stored—deep down below the waves. The Dream Machine picks out movies that tell us what's going on at the bottom of the mind-berg."

"So, what's going on at the bottom of your mind-berg, Sharon?"

"I'd sure like to know."

CHAPTER 22
THE WIND SHIFTS

Meanwhile, real life was getting worse for Sharon and her mom:

May 13: Dear Millicent, my so-called father has been home a lot. He said he was sick. He went out today, and my mother tried to call him at work and ask him to bring something home from the market. Guess what, Millicent? It turns out he doesn't work there anymore. They fired him two weeks ago.

He and my mother had another big fight when he got home. He punched her a couple of times really hard. She ran out into the front yard and he couldn't catch her, so he came back into the house and grabbed me and twisted my arm and made me yell until she came back inside. Once she was inside, he hurt her again. Then he went away. I hope I never see him again. I want him to die. That's not good, Mill.

Even though things were pretty awful for Sharon, she didn't say a lot to me about it. After school, we'd go out to the shed and look at our map and talk about what part of the world we were sailing in the *Silver Dream*. Or we'd go around the neighborhood and look for treasure. We never did find an Aladdin's lamp. They don't make them anymore. They burned oil and had little wicks. We talked and laughed about rubbing an Aladdin's flashlight instead. We figured it wouldn't be the same, though, so we decided to look for an imaginary genie bottle.

The next time Sharon and I walked along the alley behind our houses, we checked out the trash bin behind Mrs. Pinterwood's place. She throws out a lot of really good stuff because she gets tired of it or because it's dusty or cracked or something. Sometimes I think she tosses stuff out by mistake. That day, we found a funny-shaped bottle, sort of dark blue glass, with a cork in it. It was in perfect shape, the kind of bottle a genie would like to live in, I thought.

When we got home, Sharon and I cleaned the goop out of the bottle and then sat with it on the "deck" of the *Silver Dream.*

"What do you want our genie to do for you?" I asked.

Sharon frowned and said, "I want the genie to carry my father off to Arabia or Africa or a desert island somewhere, and leave him there."

"I'd like the genie to take our school away at the same time. That would save him a trip."

Sharon smiled again. "I'd like it better if the genie would help you get your homework done instead." She got down off the bench and stood in front of me.

"How can he do that?"

Sharon took me by the shoulders and shook me gently. "He'd tell you to stop playing stupid computer games and study more."

I knew she was right, but I didn't say anything. I sort of just sat there, all spaced out, feeling where she'd gripped my shoulders. I don't know what I was thinking. It took me minute before I could focus on what Sharon was saying. She waved her hand in front of my eyes to get my attention, then she patted me on the arm. "The genie says you're going to be okay, but it's not going to be easy. You'll have to be brave."

She got out the *Medal For Not Running Away,* retied the blue ribbon, and handed the medal to me. "Keep this in your pocket and remember it when you need bravery."

I wasn't so sure it would work.

Later that night, after Jason was asleep, I started up the computer. The genie's bottle was on my night table, beside the bed. I put on my thinking cap and looked up at the Now Clock. Before I could even think, my hand had grabbed the mouse and I'd started *Mind-Sweeper. Here I go again,* I thought. *What can the genie do to help me, now? What good is a genie that doesn't talk? I need somebody real! Maybe I can call Sharon . . . ? No, it's too late to call her.*

I kept on playing. A little later, I heard a noise, something creaking. *That step on the stairs!* I thought. *Here comes Dad.* I started to switch to the word processor. One keystroke would be all it took.

Then I remembered I had a *Medal For Not Running Away.*, and getting out of the game would be running away. I took the medal out and held it. *I'll let Dad catch me,* I thought. *I can just sit here and let him find out. He'll probably get mad, but he's real, and I can talk to him.* I left the game running.

Dad stuck his head into my room. "You still studying?"

"Not really."

He looked at the screen and then at me, a little surprised. "You've been playing games again?"

"I found another on my computer and I've been playing it instead of doing homework. I can't seem to stop."

"How long has this been going on?"

"Weeks."

"Weeks? David! What's got into you?"

"I don't know . . . " I looked down at the floor.

Dad stopped frowning at me and lowered his voice to keep from waking Jason. "Well, let's delete it right now."

It only took a few seconds. He fixed it so I couldn't restore the file. "I'm really surprised at you, David. This isn't like you."

My throat got all tight and I couldn't talk. I wanted to tell him how hard it was for me to do homework, even easy stuff, and how I could make myself not feel anything by starting a game. I tried, but no words would come, so I just shrugged. I felt awful.

"No wonder your grades are bad! You've been wasting all this time, with nothing to show for it."

That made me feel even more miserable. I almost started to cry then. Dad took me by the hand and said, "Okay, okay. Better late than never, David. It must have taken a lot of nerve to ask for my help. Now you'd better get some sleep. Okay?"

I nodded again, and he went downstairs. I stopped crying and tried to study, but I was way too tired. I was ashamed of myself and regretted all those lost hours. I felt like something else was gnawing a hole in me, too. I couldn't tell what it was, so I went to bed. I had some awful dreams that night.

The next day, I told Sharon what I'd done and she said she was proud of me and gave me a hug. That made me feel better for a while, but the days seemed longer and longer, after that. It was harder to get up every morning. I did study more, and I got through each day. I felt tired and sad most of the time, but I wasn't sure why. I was anxious for summer to come. For some reason, I thought everything would be better when it was summer again.

CHAPTER 23
ABSENCES

I t was late in May, a Monday morning. Rain was coming down really heavy. We waited for Sharon to show up for her lift to school, but she didn't come. I wanted to call her, but Dad said we had to leave or we'd be late.

Sharon didn't come to school at all. Her seat was empty when the bell rang. That was the first time she'd ever been late to school. I had a hard time believing she wouldn't show up before second period, for sure. I started getting a really bad feeling. I hoped she just had a cold or something.

The second period bell rang, and still no Sharon. I thought, *maybe she had to go to the doctor. She might get here at lunchtime.* As I watched the clock, I got even worrieder. *Did her dad hit her again? Is she in the hospital?*

But lunch came and went, and Sharon never came. The day seemed a million hours long. I wanted to get home and call her. I couldn't sit still. Mrs. Whitworth kept telling me to stop squirming and finally asked if I needed to go somewhere. I guess she thought I needed to take a leak. Without thinking, I looked over at Sharon's desk. Mrs. Whitworth followed my eyes, then left me alone.

When school was over, I left my umbrella behind in my rush to get out of the classroom. By the time I realized I'd forgotten it, the room was locked and it was too late to go back and get it. I waited for Grandma under the stairs beside the school to keep dry. The rain had died down to a light mist, but the wind blew it at me, and I got soaking wet. That was one of the few days when Grandma was late picking me up.

She found me there all by myself, cold and wet. "Where's Sharon?" she asked.

My teeth chattered as I told her, "She didn't come to school today."

"Are you worried about her?"

I was, but I didn't feel like I could say it, so I just shrugged and ran for the car.

When we got home, I threw my books on the kitchen table and picked up the phone. It took a long time for me to dial Sharon's number. I knew it by heart, but I was a little afraid. I hoped she'd answer, or maybe her mom would, if Sharon was sick. I didn't want to have her dad pick up the phone.

Well, that was just what happened. It rang once, and *bam*, he was on the line. He must have thought it was Sharon's mom calling, because he was yelling stuff right away, like, "Where the **** are you?" before he knew who it was. And I sure wasn't going to tell him; I hit the hang-up button with my finger and got off the phone as fast as I could. Grandma gave me a funny look.

I went upstairs and looked out my bedroom window at Sharon's house, but I couldn't see any lights on or any other sign of her. Was she home? Or had she gone someplace with her mom? Maybe they were back already. I waited a while and then decided to walk around the block and see if her mother's car was in their driveway. When I got downstairs, Grandma was on the phone, but she stopped talking. "Where are you going, David?"

"I'm going to see if Sharon is home."

"It's still raining, David. You'd better wait until later."

I went back to my room, changed into dry clothes, and put on the Thinking Cap. Then I did some homework to take my mind off

Sharon until dinner. It was sort of funny how much work I got done instead of worrying.

Dad wasn't home yet, so after dinner, I asked Grandma if I could go and check on Sharon.

Grandma put her hand on my shoulder and said, "David, Sharon will be fine."

When Dad got home a little later, he and Grandma went into the den and closed the door. After a few minutes, Dad came out and sat me down.

"What's been happening with Sharon?" he asked.

"You remember all that yelling and stuff at her house?"

"Yes."

"Her father drinks a lot and he gets drunk and breaks things. Sometimes he hits Sharon and her mom."

"I suspected that from all the noise."

"Sharon's afraid of him. She never got to school today. I tried to call her when I got home, and her father answered and started swearing. I hung up without saying anything."

"Good. Look, David, if Sharon is just sick, she'll be back in school in a day or two. In the meantime, don't try to call her on the phone."

"All right. I won't."

Dad hugged me and I felt a little better for a while. Then I started to worry again.

My homework was done, and Jason was watching TV, so I took Mom's umbrella from the front hall and went across the backyard to the *Silver Dream* to take my mind off things. I guess I hoped Sharon might come, even though it was dark and raining. I turned on the light, knelt down, and opened the "hold" to get into the secret compartment. I was going to make an entry in the log about Capt. Sharon being missing somewhere in the jungle. But when I pulled open the drawer, there was Emily looking up at me.

For a second, she looked real. I knew it was Sharon's doll, even though I'd never seen her before. It was so very strange to see her in the drawer. Then I got a really weird feeling like I'd had earlier in school, only worse.

The library books I'd checked out for Sharon were in one corner of the drawer. On top of them was a funny-shaped little rock that I'd never seen before.

I looked beneath the drawer, in the secret compartment. There was a diary on top of the *Log of the Silver Dream*, with a note.

David: Here is my diary. Please read the last entry.

I opened it and read. . .

CHAPTER 24
THE LAST LOG ENTRY

May 29: Dear David, I brought this over last night. You can read all of it, but please don't let anybody, especially my father, know you have it.

My mother and I must go away before he kills one of us. He's been getting worse when he drinks. He blacked my mother's eyes a week ago, and he's started hitting me, too.

Mother finally got it that all his excuses and promises won't stop him from doing it again. She found a place for us at a shelter. The people there said not to write or call anybody until it's safe. If he thought you'd heard from me, he'd make you tell him something that could help him find us. He might hurt you.

There's an evil thing frozen into the ice at the bottom of his mind-berg, something that thaws out when he gets drunk and makes him do awful things.

Those dreams I told you about were real. My mother had another baby when I was two. Her name was Emily, and she died at our house on Deodar Street in Los Angeles. I was old enough to miss her. To make me stop asking where she was, my mother bought me this doll, one as real as she could find, and told me it was Emily. That's why I had those dreams and used to get up and check on Emily in the middle of the night.

Now I remember Emily as a real baby, smiling and holding out a daisy to me, then reaching for me to hug her. I told these memories to my mother and asked if they were true. She started to cry and cry. *Then* she started making excuses for *him*. And that's how I know he killed Emily somehow.

I got our old house number on Deodar Street from my mother's address book. Someday I'll find where my little sister is buried. I've left the Emily doll aboard the *Silver Dream*. I'm not sure why. We have to travel light, but maybe it's more that she'd remind me too much of my real sister, or maybe I just don't need her anymore. I don't know. Please take care of her for me.

I'd like my diary back someday. I've borrowed the Ring of Truth and the Spectacles of Things as They Really Are. I need to hear the truth from my mother, and she needs to see things as they are, for a change.

These treasures will remind me of you. Especially the guardian angel pin. In exchange, I've left you something. See the *Log of the Silver Dream*.

I don't have time to say everything I want to. Some of it is here in my diary. I don't know when I'll see you again. Until then, I hope my diary and the *Log of the Silver Dream* will remind you of the good times we had.

Goodbye for now, David. Thank you for being my best friend. I'll come back someday when it's safe, I promise. — Sharon

She was gone. That awful feeling deep inside me grew until it was all through me. My eyes were all wet and blurry, and my face and my arms felt heavy. I almost couldn't move, but I put Sharon's diary safely away in the secret hiding place and slid the drawer back over it. Then I opened the *Log of the Silver Dream* to see what the last treasure was. The new entry said:

LOG OF THE SILVER DREAM, MAY 29: TODAY, AS SHE WAS PACKING, CAPT. SHARON FOUND A LOST TREASURE AMONG HER KEEPSAKES. SHE

PICKED IT UP MANY YEARS AGO ON A BEACH IN A SUNNY, FAR OFF LAND. IT LOOKS LIKE A LITTLE HEART-SHAPED ROCK, BUT IT IS ACTUALLY A TOKEN OF HER ETERNAL LOVE FOR CAPTAIN DAVID. CAPT. SHARON HAS PLACED IT HERE FOR HIM TO KEEP, AND WISHES HIM ALL THE LOVE THAT THE UNIVERSE CONTAINS, FOREVER. FAIR WINDS AND GODSPEED, DAVID!

CHAPTER 25
FALLING

It hit me then, really sank in that Sharon was *not* coming back. Part of me was still thinking, don't worry, she'll be back tomorrow or the day after. But I started crying anyway. I felt like something was being torn out of me. Why do I feel so awful? I wondered. It's not like she's dead. It's not like I'll never see her again, like Mom.

A second later, the heavy feeling spread from my arms to everywhere, and I saw the cement floor rising up at me, but I didn't seem to know what it was, or even care.

I remember nothing after that.

Later, they told me it was Jason who heard me crying, somehow, over all the rain drumming down on the roof and the patio. He told Grandma, and she and Dad came out and found me. Dad carried me inside. Grandma called Dr. Keebler, and he came over, which doctors don't do a whole lot. I don't remember any of this.

The next afternoon, I woke up in the spare bedroom. I felt really, really sad. I could tell I'd scared Dad and Grandma, which made me feel worse. Later, Dad took me to Dr. Appelman's office. It's a nice place, with wood paneling and tons of books and paintings and carvings.

And a couch. Dr. Appelman is a psychiatrist, and he's great. When he meets you, it's like he thinks you're the most important, most interesting person in the whole world. We talk a lot. Actually, he doesn't say much; he mostly listens. I told him about Sharon and how she'd gone away. I didn't cry when I told him all that. I just felt sad. But pretty soon we were talking about my mother, and I told him about my dreams where I can't find her. Then I started crying, just like the night before.

Dr. Appelman just let me cry for a long time. When I was done, he gave me some tissues to blow my nose, and we talked about grief and things. Dr. Appelman said I never got over losing my mom, and he must be right, or I wouldn't have cried. I'd pushed my feelings down where I couldn't feel them. That took a lot out of me. The dumb computer games were like my pain-killers.

On Dr. Appelman's wall, he has a little sign that says:

ONLY TEARS CAN
FREE US FROM OUR
ULTIMATE SADNESSES.

EPILOGUE

I'm better now. I'll start 7th grade in a few weeks. We moved away from "Rogersville" last summer. Dad had wanted to move right after Mom died, but our friends and Uncle Vince talked him out of doing it for a while. I'm glad they did, because I'd have had to leave Sharon before we sailed the *Silver Dream*.

We have a great little white house with a red tile roof. Grandma Greene lives in a guest house in the back. Dad has a new job and isn't working overtime anymore. He takes Jason and me and Grandma to church again, and to movies and places, the way he used to before Mom got sick. Losing Mom was really, really hard on Dad. He did the best he could, with all he had to do. He just didn't know what it was like for me. Neither did I, I guess. But things are mostly okay, now, more like they were before, except Mom is not with us.

Jason went to see Dr. Appelman, too, for a while. Jason's growing like a geranium, and he's more fun, now that he's bigger. He can play games without crying when things don't go his way. I love him a lot, and I'll never forget that he heard me crying when no one else could.

I talk to another therapist here, twice a month. I tell him about Sharon and about my Mom, and I still cry some. Not as much as at first. I don't play computer games anymore, and my last grades were almost as good as they used to be.

When we moved, Dad didn't leave a forwarding address, and we lost his company e-mail address, too. Sharon won't be able to send me a message when it's safe. I'm not sure it will be safe for a long,

long time. Before we moved, Mr. Quandres kept calling us and asking if we knew where Sharon and her mom had gone. Sometimes he was drunk and he cursed and made threats.

Dad called the police after one of those calls. I think he was afraid that Sharon's father would get violent. When we left, Dad was careful not to leave any trace that could be followed. I was even more afraid of Mr. Quandres than Dad was, because I know about Emily, the real Emily. I never told Dad about Sharon's little sister. I told Dr. Appelman, though.

I miss Sharon a lot, but I'm grateful that I knew her, and I hope I'll find her again someday. Once in a while, I have a wonderful dream where I'm on the *Silver Dream*, and Sharon is there, sailing beside me over the sapphire sea.

THE END

Resources:

Al-Anon Family Groups (AFG) is an organization of support groups for friends and relatives of alcoholics. The Al-Anon website eddress is: https://al-anon.org/

Alateen is a fellowship for young Al-Anon members. The Alateen website is at: https://al-anon.org/newcomers/teen-corner-alateen/

The information above is subject to change.

A hypothesis on the cause of alcoholism is shown in Appendix C of *In the Mouth of the Lion.* [https://www.amzn.com/dp/0997450304/].

A Final Note

I hope you've enjoyed reading *Sail Away on My Silver Dream* as much as I enjoyed writing it. But it's a fact that having written a book is more fun than writing it. And one of the very best parts of having written a book is hearing from the people who liked it! So please let me hear from you.

Better than that, even, is when readers tell other people they liked my book, either by word of mouth or in the form of a review on their favorite book discussion website. Please be one of my angels and post a review. It doesn't have to be very long.

J. Guenther's blog is found at:

https://jguentherauthor.wordpress.com/

Please stop by and leave a comment or ask a question!

Biography

J Guenther is a graduate of the University of Southern California, with BS and MS degrees in engineering. He has written 22 stage plays, three computer books, four magazine articles, 50 short stories, five novels and many poems. His classical three-act play, *Midnight in the Temple of Isis*, and many of his shorter works for the stage have been performed in theaters from Los Angeles to Santa Barbara. *Prisoner of Suggins Holler* was a prize winner in Elite Theatre Company's 2010 One-Act Play Contest. His fantasy book, *Sorcerer of Deathbird Mountain*, was nominated for best novel at the Santa Barbara Writers Conference in 2005. He has an IMDb page for acting and script consultant credits.

www.ingramcontent.com/pod-product-compliance
Lightning Source LLC
Chambersburg PA
CBHW030633130626
46552CB00002B/830